He wanted her clothes off. Wanted to feel every inch of her bare skin against his.

But a twig snapped somewhere in the distance and rational thoughts threatened to intercede. He started to pull away, but she clutched his shoulders and held him to her.

"Grace…"

She dug her nails into his back. "Shh, don't stop."

Her encouraging words tore a hole in his resistance. Hunger surged through him, raw and primal. He had to have her. Now.

He gripped the lower edge of her tank to lift it over her neck, but suddenly a popping noise echoed in the wind.

A second later, he realized the sound was gunfire, then a bullet zoomed past his head and landed at his feet.

Too close. It was time to run.

RITA HERRON

UNDER HIS SKIN

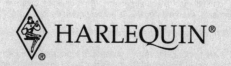

HARLEQUIN®

TORONTO • NEW YORK • LONDON
AMSTERDAM • PARIS • SYDNEY • HAMBURG
STOCKHOLM • ATHENS • TOKYO • MILAN • MADRID
PRAGUE • WARSAW • BUDAPEST • AUCKLAND

For Kim Nadelson: my former editor who still reads me
even though she doesn't have to!

ISBN-13: 978-0-373-88817-7
ISBN-10:   0-373-88817-1

UNDER HIS SKIN

ABOUT THE AUTHOR

Award-winning author Rita Herron wrote her first book when she was twelve but didn't think real people grew up to be writers. Now she writes so she doesn't have to get a *real* job. A former kindergarten teacher and workshop leader, she traded her storytelling for kids for romance, and now she writes romantic comedies and romantic suspense. She lives in Georgia with her own romance hero and three kids. She loves to hear from readers, so please write her at P.O. Box 921225, Norcross, GA 30092-1225, or visit her Web site at www.ritaherron.com.

Books by Rita Herron

HARLEQUIN INTRIGUE
790—MIDNIGHT DISCLOSURES*
810—THE MAN FROM FALCON RIDGE
861—MYSTERIOUS CIRCUMSTANCES*
892—VOWS OF VENGEANCE*
918—RETURN TO FALCON RIDGE
939—LOOK-ALIKE*
977—JUSTICE FOR A RANGER
1006—ANYTHING FOR HIS SON
1029—UP IN FLAMES*
1043—UNDER HIS SKIN*

*Nighthawk Island

Don't miss any of our special offers. Write to us at the following address for information on our newest releases.

Harlequin Reader Service
U.S.: 3010 Walden Ave., P.O. Box 1325, Buffalo, NY 14269
Canadian: P.O. Box 609, Fort Erie, Ont. L2A 5X3

CAST OF CHARACTERS

Parker Kilpatrick—He will do anything to protect Grace. Anything except give her his heart.

Grace Gardener—Someone wants to kill the nurse taking care of Parker—but why?

Bruno Gardener—Grace's brother, a local cop, supposedly committed suicide—but was his death really a murder? If so, which one of his cases got him killed?

Yvette and Jim Gardener—Grace witnessed the brutal murder of her parents twenty years ago.

Frank Johnson— This retired cop was Jim Gardener's former partner. Does he know who killed the Gardeners?

Bart Yager— An officer who worked with Jim Gardener who might know more about his friend's death than he's telling.

Juan Carlos—An ex-con who Parker suspects is trying to kill Grace.

Dr. Wilson Whitehead—The renowned doctor is interested in Grace.

Dr. Nigel Knightly—A specialist with tissue transplants.

Sonny Pradham—A lab tech at the tissue bank that supplied the hospital where Parker was treated.

Lamar Poultry—The assistant medical examiner. Is he doing more with the bodies than autopsies?

The Skulls and the Crossbones—Local gangs who are stealing corpses as pranks—or maybe it's more than just a prank.

Chapter One

Grace Gardener hesitated outside Detective Parker Kilpatrick's hospital room, nerves fluttering in her stomach. She had to find out who had murdered her brother.

The police were wrong. Bruno had not killed himself. He wouldn't take his own life. Not and leave her alone.

Ever since her parents' murder twenty years ago, she had practically raised him. And he had vowed to find out the truth about their deaths. Had that investigation gotten him killed?

Maybe Detective Kilpatrick could help her.

Although he was still recovering from the terrible fire that had put him in the hospital, he was alert, and he could ask around.

She had to be careful and guard her emotions, though. For some insane reason, the detective rattled her nerves. But she refused to get involved with a detective, not after losing two loved ones to the job.

For heaven's sake, he'd only been with the Savannah Police Department a short time and he'd ended up at death's door, and now in the hospital.

With a shudder, she remembered the night they'd wheeled Parker into the ER. He'd been injured trying to save a woman's life in a fire. A hero, but he'd suffered second- and third-degree burns, had a collapsed lung and crushed leg. Had nearly flatlined. She'd held his hand and called to him, urging him to fight for his life, and miraculously they'd revived him.

And when he'd opened his amber eyes and looked at her, even glazed with pain, she'd felt an odd chemistry between them. A chemistry she hadn't felt with a man in a long time.

She clenched her hands; she was the delirious one. She'd simply connected to him because of his close call with death, the excitement of bringing him back and knowing that she would play a part in his recovery.

But he'd barked at her over the next few weeks and thrown her out of his room more than once, refusing her help. Still, she'd held on to her patience because she'd understood his frustration.

He was an alpha male who liked being in charge, and he'd been robbed of his independence. Her brother and father had been tough as nails like him, and would have responded the same way to being physically incapacitated.

Remembering them again sobered her, so she knocked on the door. When she heard his gruff voice, she stepped inside. For a brief moment she paused, her breath catching at the sight of him standing on his own. He was over six feet and had powerful shoulders, now encased in a dark blue T-shirt that emphasized his muscular physique. Thick, wavy dark brown hair framed an angular face constantly darkened by beard stubble, and though a scar ran along his temple, his face, thank God, had not suffered burns.

She remembered seeing him half-naked when she'd tended to him, and her stomach quivered. Even in a hospital gown, he was the best-looking masculine specimen she'd ever met. She'd wanted to soothe his pain, to heal him with her hands, and had admired his fierce determination and insistence that the doctors were wrong, that he'd show them all and walk again.

"What are you doing here?"

A small smile tilted her lips at his surly tone. "Nice to see you, too, Parker. I just dropped by to check on your progress."

His jaw tightened, and a flicker of something that resembled pain flared in his eyes as he walked toward her. He wasn't using the crutches, although he probably should be. "I'm fine, as you can see. Now you can go."

"Ah. I forgot you don't like company."

"I'm a cop, not into chitchat."

Right, the cop part. He was antsy to get back to the job. To put his life on the line again to save others.

And possibly end up right back here or worse, dead like her brother and father. She still didn't understand what drove them to put themselves in danger, and make their loved ones worry and suffer.

She spotted the newspaper on the bed, noted the story about the missing bodies from the morgues and the story about the body she'd found at the graveyard the night before when she'd stopped by to visit Bruno's grave.

Nightmares of the man's blank eyes staring at her in death haunted her all night. "I see you're keeping up with the crime in Savannah."

For a moment concern warmed his eyes. "Yeah, I saw the story. Are you all right?"

She nodded, moved by the slight tenderness in his husky voice. "I hope they find whoever left his body. That poor man didn't deserve to be desecrated like that."

"My partner's on the case. He'll get to the bottom of it."

She tucked an errant strand of hair behind one ear. He'd just given her an opener. "I spoke with Captain Black about my brother's death. But he said they still don't know anything. And I'm not convinced that he believes me."

He shrugged, drawing the T-shirt tighter across his massive chest while the cotton running shorts he wore slid down to reveal his flat stomach. Dark hair was broken by patches that had been singed off, and scars discolored the bronzed skin, but they were healing.

"Captain Black is a good guy. He's trying to find out the truth, Grace. So what are you really doing here?"

She stared at him for a long moment, debating over whether to leave or ask for his help like she'd originally intended. If she did ask, would he tell her to stay out of it as his captain had, or would he help her?

PARKER SILENTLY CURSED himself for his rudeness. Grace Gardener had dragged him back from the brink of death, and while he'd been trapped like a sick animal in ICU, her gentle hands had tended to his injuries and helped him with routine tasks that no man wanted a woman's help with.

The very reason he could barely look her in the face.

He wanted her bad. Wanted her like a man wanted a woman. To strip her clothes, feel her curvy body naked and writhing beneath his. Wanted to hear that sultry voice whispering his name in the heat of passion, not sympathy.

Yet she'd seen him at his most vulnerable. Thought of him as the poor, sick, scarred, crippled man who needed to lean on her small frame just to walk to the damn bathroom.

A big man like him shouldn't be leaning on anyone, much less a female half his size.

The reason he had to get rid of her. If she stayed much longer, looking so soft and sweet, making him need her in other ways than as a physical crutch, he'd make a fool out of himself.

"Go home, Grace. You helped patch me up, your job is over."

She nodded. "I just wanted to see how the leg was doing."

His mouth thinned but he shrugged. "I'll be jogging out of here soon."

She laughed softly. "I'm sure you will."

The conviction in her voice offered him hope just as her comforting words in the ER had. As if to contradict him though, his leg suddenly seized up. A sharp agonizing pain split his calf and bolted up toward his spine, and sweat broke out all over his body. He felt dizzy and gritted his teeth, praying she'd leave before he did something embarrassing like pass out on her. Or end up on the floor where he'd have to crawl back to the bed.

She obviously saw the pain he desperately tried to hide, and eased toward him. "Sit down, Parker. You've probably been overdoing it again with your therapy."

He had been pushing himself beyond the requirements but was determined to get back on his feet, literally.

The pain intensified, the room growing fuzzy. In spite of his resolve, he gripped the metal rail of the bed to steady himself and tried to move toward it. She was beside him in a flash, slid one hand beneath his arm and helped him take the agonizing steps back to the bed. She said nothing as he lowered himself onto the mattress, but when he tried to lift his injured leg to stretch it out, the muscles were so knotted and bunched, that he had to bend over to work out the spasm. She stooped and began to massage the muscle, her fingers deftly working magic. Then she helped him straighten his leg on the bed. Her eyes met his for a brief moment, and she offered a tentative smile, then once again kneaded his cramped calf.

He clenched his jaw to keep from moaning and wiped sweat from his upper lip, battling the need to order her to stop, but her hands felt so damn wonderful that he couldn't bear to ask her to quit. Like he had so many other times, he wanted those hands on him in other places. Places that hadn't been touched in forever.

You're a weak man, his father had told him as he'd tried to beat some sense into him.

Damn it, he was right. And Parker hated it.

A knock sounded at the door and one of the surgeons who'd operated on Parker, a lean, ash-blond man named Dr. Wilson Whitehead, poked his head in. He glanced at Grace and his brows arched as if he was surprised to see her in the room, especially sitting on the side of his bed rubbing Parker's leg.

"Parker?"

Parker pushed Grace's hands away and crossed his arms. She stood, a flash of contrition in her eyes as if she'd been caught behaving unprofessionally when she'd simply been doing her job.

"Grace?"

She nodded in greeting. "Dr. Whitehead."

Again, a look of question darkened his eyes, and Parker's senses jumped to alert. The doctor was interested in Grace. Were they involved?

Humiliation crawled up his spine for even thinking she might be attracted to him. A gorgeous woman like her probably had men chasing her all the time. Healthy men like Dr. Whitehead with a boatload of money, men who could wine and dine her, not a scarred guy with a bad attitude and a life that had no room for anything but tracking criminals. A job that would only put her in danger.

"What's going on?" Parker asked.

Dr. Whitehead stepped farther into the room and approached the bed. His gray eyes bore into Parker's, serious and filled with the same professional detached expression that he wore when he'd informed Parker he'd never walk again.

He had bad news. Just how bad?

Parker's patience disintegrated. "I asked you what the hell is going on."

Dr. Whitehead stuffed his hands in the pockets of his white lab coat. "I've reviewed your last tests, and they're not good. You're not healing as well with the new tendons as I'd expected."

Not news to him. He wanted to heal faster, too.

"I've just learned that we have a tissue recall," the doctor continued. "The tissue you received is part of that recall."

"What's wrong with the tissue?" Parker asked.

"It wasn't processed properly. That may be the reason for your lack of progress."

"So this new tissue might work better?"

"Exactly."

"This means another surgery?"

"Yes, another transplant."

Parker grimaced, the reality setting in. More surgery meant an extended hospital stay, a longer recovery. More rehab.

A more lengthy leave of absence before he could return to work and be a whole man.

He cut his gaze toward Grace and wondered if she'd known, if she'd come because she felt sorry for him and wanted to see how he'd handle the news.

Not because she liked him personally.

Hell, he'd take the surgery if it meant a chance his leg might recover.

But he wouldn't accept Grace's pity or delude himself into thinking that she might be attracted to him—not ever again.

Chapter Two

Grace saw the wheels turning in Parker's head. Frustration lined his face, as well as pain, and the realization of what another surgery meant.

A setback in his recovery.

Yet the hope that the unhealthy tissue was the reason for his slow progress also glittered in his eyes. And the bad tissue had to be removed. That was a given.

He angled his face toward the doctor. "Do you really think this surgery will make a difference?"

Dr. Whitehead gave a clipped nod. "Yes. The contaminated tissue most likely caused the irritation in your leg, the constant discomfort and the subsequent infection."

Parker seemed to assimilate the doctor's

comments, then he released a heavy sigh full of resignation. "All right, when do we do it?"

"The sooner, the better. How about first thing in the morning?"

"Fine. Let's get it over with."

Dr. Whitehead nodded. "I'll talk to the nurses and make sure they have you prepped and ready."

He grimaced. "Great."

Dr. Whitehead turned to her. "Grace?"

"Yes?"

"Walk out with me?"

"Sure. Just give me a minute."

Parker's amber eyes pierced her. "Go, Grace. Guess I'd better rest up before the next carving."

Her heart squeezed for him. But how many times did he have to tell her to leave before she got the message?

Besides, how could he help her now? He would need rest, to recuperate…

She was on her own.

"All right. Good luck tomorrow." She offered him an encouraging smile. "I'll stop by to check on you."

"Don't bother."

"It's my job," she said defensively. Although she knew she was lying. There were other nurses just as capable. She didn't have to follow up on his recovery, didn't have to visit him. Didn't have to even think about him once he left her care.

But occasionally a patient got under her skin. And while she'd tended to Parker, she'd started to care for him. She not only wanted his help with her brother's case, but she wanted to see him heal, to regain full use of his leg, because she admired him. She'd never seen a patient so determined to beat the odds and regain his mobility. Any part she played in that progress gave her a sense of accomplishment.

He picked up the newspaper, effectively cutting her off, and she sighed. The most difficult cases were the most challenging, but the most rewarding.

But she wouldn't throw herself at the man, not when as soon as he recovered, he'd return to the police force. To a job that she hated. One that would most likely get him killed.

So she left the room, shutting the door behind her.

"I was surprised to find you visiting Parker Kilpatrick," Wilson said.

Grace hesitated. The doctor had expressed interest in her more than once. Had hinted at lunch a couple of times, but she'd managed to avoid a direct rejection.

"I like to follow up on my patients," she said.

"Are you sure it isn't because he's a cop?"

His question rubbed her the wrong way. He knew she'd suffered over her brother's death. "I take my job very seriously, Dr. Whitehead. Parker has had a tough go of it, and I want to see him make a full recovery."

"I didn't mean to offend you, Grace. You're a wonderful nurse." His smile softened. "That's one of the qualities I admire most about you. That and your legs."

Buttering her up with a compliment should have made her feel good. Instead she took a step backward. Although she normally didn't date people she worked with, she had entertained the idea of going out with him.

But a few moments earlier, when she'd seen him standing beside Parker, she had been drawn to Parker instead. Even though he was injured, struggling to recover, and had scars, Wilson Whitehead paled in comparison.

"How about dinner?" he asked.

She shook her head. "No, thanks. I'm really tired tonight."

"Grace—"

"Maybe another time, Wilson." She rubbed her temple, feigning a headache. "I'd better go." She rushed away before he could respond.

She was tired, and wanted to get to bed early for the morning shift. Whether Parker wanted her nearby for his surgery or not, she intended to be there.

And if he did recover, maybe he'd take her brother's case. Until then, she had to dig around on her own.

PARKER CURSED as Grace shut the door. Damn it, he shouldn't have been so brusque, but knowing she'd seen him at his weakest was more than he could bear. And now the thought of undergoing another surgery, more rehab....

He slammed his fist into his pillow, wanting to vent his rage.

But he'd been taught control, he had to exert it now. Irritated at himself for his outburst, he reined in his temper. He refused to give in to despair.

He would endure the surgery, the pain afterward, then walk again, and he'd do it without those cursed crutches.

Maybe the contaminated tissue had impeded his recovery, and this new surgery would do the trick. Then he could resume his life.

He was nothing without his work.

Frustrated at the fact that he couldn't help with the body-snatcher investigation, he hobbled off the bed, then slowly shuffled over to the small desk in the corner of the room. At least the rehab facility at the Coastal Island Research Park offered more than a plain hospital room, and they had wireless Internet services. Since many of the patients required long-term care, the center encouraged patients to continue their work if possible, and had provided accommodations to ensure that possibility through modern technology.

He booted up the computer, then accessed the police databases and searched for stories about the missing corpses to see if there were other similar cases in the South or across the States. Several cropped up, so he methodically accessed each one.

The stories of necromancy made his skin crawl—two had occurred in Savannah four years earlier, three in Atlanta, and numerous others in New Orleans and across the States. Most had been solved, although one case in the hills of North Carolina had never been closed.

A satanic cult in the Tennessee mountains had also stolen bodies to burn as a sacrifice. A case in eastern Kentucky noted a serial killer who dismembered corpses after he killed the victims—the killer had been tried and convicted, and was now on death row.

Some bodies had been stolen from morgues around Halloween for pranks. Other cases involved stealing comatose patients for organs to sell on the black market.

A schizophrenic man in North Carolina had stolen corpses because he swore he heard voices telling him to turn them into vampires.

He paused, rubbed his hand over his face. Even though he'd been a cop for years, the depravity of humans still stunned him.

Having read about the questionable projects a few doctors had been involved with at CIRP, he ran a search for medical purposes for which a corpse could be used. Research experiments and medical educational facilities topped the list. But those bodies were donated to science, not stolen. There was no report indicating they had a shortage of donors for either.

Knowing any one of the above could be the motive for the current body snatcher, or that they might be dealing with yet a different scenario, he made a note of the various motives.

One of the nurses poked her head in. "Mr. Kilpatrick?"

"Yes?"

"Dr. Whitehead suggested I give you a sleeping pill to help you relax before your surgery tomorrow."

"I don't need a pill."

She shrugged. "All right, but I'll be in to get you bright and early."

Her cheerful smile irritated him. "Fine. I'll be here," he mumbled. As if he'd be anywhere else.

He checked the morgues housing the bodies for reports of impropriety but found nothing. In spite of his resolve to work, exhaustion wore on him. Another downside of his injuries; he'd yet to regain his stamina. And he would need his energy to force himself to endure the agonizing therapy following tomorrow's ordeal.

Within seconds after his head hit the pillow he faded into sleep, but images of Grace's blue eyes flashed into his mind. He didn't need her at his side, but he couldn't help but wish she'd show up anyway. Just hearing her voice before he went under the knife would give him comfort.

DARK STORM CLOUDS HOVERED in the sky, obliterating the moon and stars as Grace drove to Tybee Island and the cottage her parents had owned. Thunder rumbled and lightning crisscrossed the darkness above the palm trees, signs of an impending storm.

Grace hated storms. There had been a terrible one the night her parents died.

Worse, all the Halloween decorations in town and on the island reminded her of the ghost stories and legends of pirates and lost souls in the area, adding to her paranoia.

She tried to focus on the reason she'd moved back to the cottage—because it was so peaceful. She craved the lulling sound of the ocean in the background, the warm fall air, the smell of the marsh and the sway of the palm trees in the late-night breeze. During the summer months when most of the cottages were inhabited, either

by homeowners or renters, the island
came alive with bikers, joggers, walkers
and children. But fall sent vacationers
home, and the island felt isolated, even
deserted and eerie at times.

Especially at the end of the street tucked
back into the cove where she lived.

Tonight, in light of the ghouls and
goblins hanging on door fronts and trees,
the recent wave of vandalism and stories
of missing corpses, she felt on edge, as if
someone was watching her. Someone who
was waiting in the shadows, ready to leap
out and grab her.

Maybe she shouldn't have returned to
her parents' home. It had stirred all kinds
of memories. But pleasant ones mingled
with the sad. The rare times when her father
had taken vacation days, rented a fishing
boat and taken her and Bruno fishing in the
inlet. The crabbing expeditions in the
marsh. The long walks on the beach searching for sea turtles and shells. Building sand
sculptures and flying kites in the spring.

Although her parents hadn't died in this
house, she thought about them more and
more since she'd returned.

She parked in the clamshell drive, lifted her hair off her neck to let the breeze brush her skin as she let herself in the cottage. The wind chimes on the front porch tinkled, and inside, lavender and cinnamon scented the air. Remembering the figure running into the woods the night before at the graveyard, she paused in the doorway, listening for an intruder. What if the man in the woods thought she had seen him?

What if he came looking for her?

Chapter Three

Shivering, Grace flipped on the TV and checked the news while she ate a salad. Maybe they'd found the culprit and he was in jail now.

The report was already midway: "Tonight, we've had another case of what the police believe to be vandalism." The camera panned to a cemetery outside of town. "Someone flooded the graveyard by Shiloh Church, saturating the ground so badly that several feet of dirt washed away and caskets have risen to the surface. A Halloween prank or is someone robbing graves now?"

Grace frowned and waited to see if they mentioned the corpse from the night before, but the reporter spent most of the segment on interviews at the church scene. Sighing, she chided herself for worrying, took her salad plate to the sink, rinsed it and stuck it in the dishwasher, then stepped outside on the back patio. The smell of the marsh assaulted her, and the sound of the ocean crashing against the shore filled her ears. But thunder rattled her nerves, and the wind brought the whisper of her brother's voice.

"Help me…"

She froze. She must have imagined the words, had been thinking about Bruno too much lately because of these missing corpses.

That and the fact that his killer had never been caught.

Suddenly exhausted, she went back inside, stripped her clothes and slipped into a cool, cotton nightshirt. For a brief moment she allowed herself to think about Parker Kilpatrick, and imagined him beside her, watching her undress. Imagined him smiling as he ran his hands over her bare breasts. Imagined him erasing thoughts of dead bodies and replacing them with an erotic night of lovemaking.

But the image of his frown when he'd told her to leave returned, drowning out the fantasy, and she crawled into bed, reminding herself that nothing could happen between them.

He was a cop. She'd lost her mother and the two most important men in her life, everyone she had ever loved, to the job, and she refused to take the chance on that again. Besides, he wasn't interested in her.

Feeling claustrophobic, she left the window open so she could feel the breeze and hear the waves during the night and soon fell into a deep sleep.

But rest didn't come. Instead nightmares of her childhood did.

THE STORM RAGED outside, shaking the walls and beating the thin windowpanes. She was seven years old, huddled in bed with her teddy bear, trying to drown out the noise by covering her ears with her hands. Her little brother had gone to a friend's for the night, and she wanted to climb in bed with her parents, but her daddy told her earlier she had to be a big girl.

Her chin wobbled as she fought tears. Suddenly a loud boom split the air. The storm?

It sounded like thunder. No...someone had screamed.

Her heart pounding, she slipped from bed and padded toward the door to the den. Mommy would hold her and make everything all right. Would keep her safe from the storm, and tell her the screams were all in her head.

But when she peered through the crack in the door to the den, she saw her parents hovering together on the sofa. Her mommy was crying.

Then she saw the other man. A big guy in black clothes with a ski mask over his face. He was waving a gun at her parents.

Another streak of lightning fell across the room and he shoved her father back onto the sofa and pointed the gun at his head.

Her mother screamed, then a gunshot

*blasted the air. Blood splattered the floor
and walls. Grace closed her eyes and sank
to the floor in horror, then covered her
ears as a second shot blasted.*

*Without looking she knew her parents
were dead.*

TIME TO GO under the knife.

Parker grimaced as the first strains of
daylight stole into the hospital room. In
spite of his resolve not to get involved
with Grace Gardener, he searched the
faces of the nurses for her sea-blue eyes.
Another nurse prepped him for surgery
and when she started to give him a shot to
relax him before they transported him to
the operating room, he finally accepted
that Grace wasn't coming.

She had given up on being his friend.
He'd driven her away.

Good. He didn't need or want her
hovering over him. Doing him any favors.
Smiling at him like he meant something
special to her when she probably treated
all her patients the same way.

Besides, he knew she wanted answers

about her brother's death. Answers he didn't have. As soon as he'd joined the precinct, the serial arsonist had struck and he and his partner had been swamped with the case.

But when he got back on track, he'd investigate and see what he could find out about Bruno's death. All he'd heard when he'd replaced the investigating cop was that Bruno had committed suicide, although some of the locals suspected he hadn't killed himself. He'd been found with a bullet in his head and had fallen over a cliff. They wouldn't have a body if a storm hadn't washed it back in. Which made him suspicious.

That was probably the *only* reason Grace had been so friendly. She wanted his help.

Still, he felt a tug of disappointment in his chest that she hadn't dropped by to see him this morning. Hadn't he learned? People only used you when they needed something. Promises were only words that were broken.

The medicine kicked in and his head

became fuzzy, the room a kaleidoscope of beige on white that swirled in a drunken haze.

Suddenly two blue circles appeared in the haze. Grace's smiling eyes. Then her angelic voice penetrated the fog, calling his name.

"You're going to do great, Parker," she whispered. "And when this is over, you'll heal just like you want. One day you'll walk out of here and we'll never see you again."

He smiled, or at least he thought he did. His face felt funny, as if it was melting clay, and his lips seemed gluey, his tongue thick as if it was swollen inside his mouth.

"I'll see you when you wake up." She squeezed his hand and he tried to squeeze back to let her know he heard, that he appreciated her visit, but he didn't know if he'd actually moved his fingers.

Then they were rolling him into a room with bright lights. The operating room. A mask slid over his face. Faces blurred, voices became a rumbling echo, distant and indiscernible.

Slowly the world faded into nothingness, where he dreamed about death. He was being buried but someone had stolen his body from the casket…

GRACE TRIED NOT TO WORRY about Parker during the surgery—after all, this was routine compared to the condition he'd been in when he'd first been admitted. But something about the tissue recalls disturbed her.

What exactly was the problem with the initial tissues? Although the hospital was affiliated with CIRP and took advantage of all the cutting-edge techniques, it had an impeccable reputation. The area had become a hubbub of high-tech medical research, and patients came from all over the States to utilize the latest treatments available. Sometimes in desperation, they agreed to new treatments offered through the research projects as a last resort.

But these tissue transplants were fairly common. Perhaps the problem wasn't with the hospitals but with the tissue banks.

She spent the morning tending to other patients, and when the orderlies wheeled Parker to ICU after he was released from recovery, she rushed to check on his condition. He was breathing fine, his vitals were normal, and he had come through the surgery with flying colors. He didn't need her, just a nurse to take care of routine tasks.

So why did she stay close to his side all morning? Why did she run every time she heard his breathing turn erratic or hear him moan in pain?

Furious with herself, she allowed another nurse to help him walk the first time. And when they transported him to a regular room, she was relieved. No more making a fool of herself over the man. He was on his own.

Still, the questions concerning the tissue transplants needled her. When she stepped into the hospital lounge for a midmorning cup of coffee, two surgical nurses hovered together in low conversation. "So far, we've had at least twenty patients affected," one of the nurses said.

"The hospital will get flack for this," the other nurse muttered.

"I just hope the police don't ask questions," the first nurse said.

"Why would they?"

"With this many patients involved, and with one of them a cop, the press will have a heyday. There'll probably be lawsuits."

Suddenly they spotted her and clammed up. But the rest of the morning, their conversation haunted Grace.

When she slipped into the hospital cafeteria for lunch, she spotted Dr. Whitehead and his colleague Dr. Nigel Knightly in deep conversation. She grabbed a chicken salad sandwich and a glass of sweet tea, half hoping to avoid Wilson Whitehead, but he cornered her and insisted she join them for lunch.

Dr. Knightly had performed Parker's surgery so she decided to broach the subject of the tissue transplant with him. "The surgery with Parker Kilpatrick went okay?"

"Yes, it was a success," Dr. Knightly said.

"This tissue was checked prior to

surgery so we don't expect any more problems," Dr. Whitehead added.

She sipped her tea. "Did you get any more details on the recalled tissue?"

Dr. Knightly shrugged. "It wasn't processed properly after extraction. That causes infection, rejection in some cases, and in one case now the patient has reacted, become septic and a limb had to be amputated."

"Where do you think the problem originated?" she asked, digging for more information.

Dr. Whitehead arched his blond brows. "Why are you so interested, Grace?"

"Patients ask questions," she replied quickly. "Sometimes they're afraid or hesitant to go to the doctors. I just want to be prepared."

He studied her for a long moment as if assessing the truth of her statement, then offered a small smile. "The problem didn't occur in our hospital, that's for sure. Probably an inexperienced or sloppy lab technician who didn't know what he was doing."

And since more than one hospital received tissue from designated tissue banks, other facilities and patients might be affected. "Then the problems might be far more widespread than our hospital here. Have the necessary parties been notified?" Grace asked.

The doctors exchanged an odd look, then Dr. Whitehead covered her hand with his. "Yes. Now, don't worry yourself over this, Grace. We have the situation under control."

She tensed at his patronizing tone. And the strange look in Dr. Knightly's eyes sent a tingle of nerves up her spine. They obviously didn't want her asking questions about the transplants.

THE NEXT WEEK passed in a blur of pain, physical therapy and frustration for Parker. Not wanting to grow addicted to the medication, by midweek he refused the pain pills.

By Friday, his leg felt remarkably better than after the first surgery.

He walked the halls with the help of

one crutch instead of two, and hoped to be transferred to the rehab facility soon.

The only downside to the transfer was that he wouldn't get to see Grace every day. Pathetic though it was, he looked forward to the five-minute, drop-in visits that she'd carved out of her busy day for him.

Unfortunately while he'd been laid up, several more bodies had been stolen from different morgues, two of which were involved in pranks. Three others had gone missing, only to be discovered later at a different morgue or funeral home. The coroner's office had argued improper tagging and blamed a shoddy body-moving service.

Tests were being run to see if any trace evidence had been left on the bodies.

He'd also heard whispers about other patients being brought in for tissue replacement surgeries. One man had died from an infection.

He shuddered, knowing he should be grateful. And he wanted to repay Grace by finding out the truth about her brother's death.

Dark storm clouds cast a gray fog over the sky, the rolling thunderstorms mirroring his mood. He hadn't been out in days and missed the sunshine on his face and the fresh air.

The barometric pressure seemed to affect his knee and made it ache. Thunder burst into a roar, and the power flickered off then back on, making him think about the hospital and potential problems if a power shortage occurred. Backup generators would kick in, but what if they lost a patient during the time that took?

Funny how he never considered those issues before he'd been imprisoned in the facility. He had too damn much time to think. Which he'd been doing a lot of. The problems with the tissue banks disturbed him. He'd heard rumors that one of the doctors might have known about the problems but used the tissue anyway.

He was taking a final spin around the hospital wing when he spotted Grace approaching him. She looked tired and agitated but so beautiful his gut tightened, and arousal speared him. At least that part

of him hadn't been injured. The only plea-
surable sensation he'd experienced lately.

Unfortunately he couldn't assuage the
ache.

He had to spend all his time and energy
on getting better. Returning to his job was
all that mattered.

HE CHECKED the toe tags on the stiffs in the
crypt, choosing the one that had been pre-
ordained for his mission, a John Doe. It was
past midnight, the place was deserted, and
although corpses didn't faze him, being
inside the cold room alone at night
reminded him of the chilling stories his
grandmother told about ghosts rising from
the dead.

The heavy scent of formaldehyde and
other chemicals blended into the icy air,
the shadows casting ominous shades of
gray across the chalky-white pallor of
the deceased. Sometimes he thought he
heard their voices calling from the steel
tables, heard whispers of lost ones trying
to rise again.

Dressed in surgical scrubs, he blended

in with the other staff members as he zipped up the body bag and pushed the gurney through the side door for transport by the body movers.

There would be no rest for him tonight, though. He had work to do and only hours to perform his tasks. He'd better get started.

Chapter Four

Parker sucked in a sharp breath and walked toward Grace, proud of his progress, that he could stand upright instead of having to look up at her from a hospital bed. He'd also asked Bradford Welsh, his partner, to get him Bruno's file so he could study it while he was recuperating.

"You look amazing," Grace said.

He nodded, pride filling him. "The leg is feeling better."

"Obviously the healthy tissue made a huge difference."

Something about her tone disturbed him. "Yes. I guess I'm one of the lucky ones."

She frowned. "You heard about some of the other patients?"

He nodded. "One dead of infection, and three lost limbs."

Her eyes flickered with worry. "That never should have happened."

He frowned. "What's wrong, Grace?"

She glanced around the nurses' station, then lowered her voice. "Are you up for a walk to the coffee machine?"

He'd pushed himself to the limit with his therapy this morning, and his leg was throbbing, but damned if he'd admit it. "Sure."

She began walking down the hall, obviously slowing her gait to match his. Irritation nagged at him, but he wrestled it under control. "Okay, what's on your mind?" he asked as they settled in a deserted corner with coffee.

"I probably shouldn't say anything. The hospital staff doesn't want gossip."

"Did someone ask you to keep quiet?"

"Not exactly. But I can't help but wonder if someone here knew the tissue was faulty and used it anyway."

He sighed. Hadn't he wondered the same thing? "You have a name?"

She shook her head. "Nothing definite, just hints here and there. Everyone is very hush-hush."

"That's no surprise. They're probably concerned about lawsuits."

"And criminal charges now with this man's death," she murmured.

"What do you think happened, Grace?" he asked bluntly.

Her troubled gaze met his, then she took a long sip of her coffee. "I'm not sure. We get the tissue from tissue banks. One of the physicians said he thinks that's where the breakdown occurred. It was processed improperly, probably by a technician who didn't know what he was doing."

"But you have another theory?"

"His speculation makes perfect sense. But those missing corpses have me perplexed. I know some have been used in pranks for Halloween, but the others…"

His skin prickled. "What about them?"

"Sometimes we have live donors, but often tissue is taken from the deceased."

Suspicion twitched at him. "You think

the missing corpses are being used to extract tissue?"

"I don't know, Parker, it's just a thought." She chewed her bottom lip. "There's something else. When my brother was killed, his body went missing for two days. Eventually it turned up at a different morgue. The coroner said that it was a clerical error, but now I'm wondering…"

"Wouldn't the autopsies show if tissue was removed?"

"Yes, although some tissue might be removed after the autopsy."

"Didn't the ME check the bodies after they were recovered?"

"Yes." She sighed. "I guess I'm just going off on a tangent. Trying to find something that isn't there."

"Like the fact that you don't believe your brother killed himself?"

She gave him a withering look. "I *know* Bruno wouldn't take his own life. The bullet in the head sounds like a professional hit to me. Maybe he was investigating some kind of mob crime."

"Grace, I saw Bruno's file. He left a suicide note. They analyzed the handwriting and it matched your brother's—"

"Someone could have forced him to write that, and you know it." She knotted her hands in her lap so tightly her knuckles turned white. "And then for his body to go missing…"

"What did the coroner say after they recovered his body? Had it been mishandled?"

She reluctantly shook her head. "They said it hadn't."

Parker twisted his mouth in thought. Unless the police hadn't told her. Sometimes they withheld details of a crime from the family and press to use later in case of an arrest.

Besides, if she was right and her brother hadn't committed suicide, then she might also be correct about the hit.

"My partner thinks there's a group of teens stealing the bodies," Parker said. "He found a pentagram painted on the lawn of a local church, and dead animals left around it. They may be using the

corpses in some kind of ritualistic cere-
mony."

"I read something about that in the
paper," she admitted. "Sounds feasible."

Parker wanted to console her, but didn't
know how. Not unless he found the truth.
"I've requested the police reports on your
brother's death."

Her gaze jerked to his. "Did you find
anything?"

"Not yet," he said quietly. "But I'll find
out what happened to him, Grace. I promise."

The relief in her eyes made his chest
squeeze, although guilt plagued him.
Family members always wanted to deny
that one of their loved ones would commit
suicide, but it happened. Men, even cops,
folded under pressure.

He wanted to reach out and touch her,
but he didn't dare. Because touching her
once wouldn't be enough.

And he had no illusions that she wanted
anything from him but answers about her
brother's case. After all, he was weak. A
scarred man.

Lying in bed helpless he might have fantasized about having a woman in his life on a permanent basis.

But when he returned to the job, that was not an option.

THUNDER POPPED OUTSIDE, and lightning crackled, streaking the dark sky with jagged lines that jarred Grace from her seat.

She wrapped her arms around her waist, then glanced at Parker and saw him watching her. Good heavens, she must look like a ninny.

Still she moved away from the window. Tried to forget that all week she'd felt as if someone was following her. That she wondered if the man she'd seen in the woods at the graveyard might be after her.

If the person who'd killed her brother might want her dead because she wouldn't leave the case alone.

She wanted to confide in Parker, but the man had enough on his plate right now. He would probably think she was paranoid if she confessed her fears.

At least he was going to look into her brother's death.

Not that he could do a lot while recovering, but he could ask questions, maybe convince his partner to help him. She certainly hadn't gotten anywhere on her own.

Curious about the tissue banks and the possibility of a cover-up, she decided to dig around a little after she walked Parker back to his room. She'd subtly questioned other nurses and Dr. Whitehead again, but he assured her that the hospital administrator was investigating the matter and would inform them of the results when he found the source of the problem.

So why did she sense they were hiding the truth?

Having a cop for a brother and father must have made her suspicious of everything. She didn't trust anyone.

Parker's face materialized, but she reminded herself that he was a detective, as well. Cops kept secrets, even from people they cared about. Her brother had. And so had her father.

Those secrets had gotten them killed.

Remembering the body she'd seen in the graveyard and the figure in the woods, she shivered. He'd been painted so grotesquely that he was probably part of a prank, but still the police weren't sure. And they weren't telling her anything.

Maybe she could sneak into records and find the man's autopsy. Maybe she'd find Bruno's and check it out, as well. She especially wanted to see the report the coroner had filed after Bruno's body had been recovered.

Unable to rest for the questions needling her, she headed toward the records department. A crowd filled the elevator, so she waited for another. But the power blinked off, then on again, and she panicked. No way she'd get trapped in the elevator, so she darted into the stairwell.

She'd made it to the second-floor landing when the sound of something scraping broke the silence. She froze, her breathing vibrating in the quiet. Was someone in the stairwell with her? Maybe behind her?

She turned to look, but the lights blinked off again, pitching her into darkness. She swallowed hard as thunder roared, and prayed the lights would be restored immediately. But the stairwell remained cloaked in a black fog. The scent of some kind of chemical and stale air permeated the space. Then the sound of a shoe padding softly on cement broke the silence. Someone was in the stairwell with her, and they were coming toward her.

"Who's there?" she called.

No answer.

The hair on the nape of her neck stood on end, and she called out, but again no answer. The footsteps drew closer, louder. Ominous.

Panicking, she gripped the handrail and began to feel her way down the steps. One step, two, three, her heel caught the edge and she stumbled. Her heart pounding, she grabbed the rail and steadied herself, breathing heavy. The footsteps sped up.

She had to hurry. But the whisper of a breath bathed her neck, then someone shoved her from behind.

She screamed, clawing for the railing, but her hands connected only with air.

Then she lost her balance and went careening down the staircase.

Chapter Five

Grace's questions about the tissue transplants aroused Parker's curiosity. Although Bradford had informed him about the Coastal Island Research Park and some unethical projects that had taken place, stealing dead bodies to remove tissues seemed far-fetched. Captain Black and Detective Clayton Fox had investigated the center for over a year. Fox had gotten too close to one case and they'd performed a memory transplant on him. For months he'd actually believed he was a guy named Cole.

Police had also exposed another experiment where children had been trained and brainwashed to be spies. A twin identity experiment had taken one of the participant's lives, and a few months back, someone had poisoned unsuspecting people with a chemical that caused depression, delusions, agoraphobia, and eventually lead to suicide. Bradford's wife and brother had also been subjects of a study on paranormal abilities.

Then again, the painted corpses definitely read like teenage pranks.

But worry nagged at him. He didn't like the fact that the paper had printed Grace's name as a possible witness to a crime. Or that they'd revealed that she was pushing the police to find her brother's killer.

Besides, a cop would most likely eat his gun versus a bullet to his temple.

He had to know more about Bruno's cases.

The bullet to the head fit the MO of a professional hit. Or had the killer meant to make it look that way?

Grace's conviction that her brother had been murdered drove him to pick up the file Bradford had dropped off earlier. He flipped it open and began trying to decipher the man's handwriting to review his past cases. Someone Bruno had arrested might have harbored a vendetta against him.

Parker jotted down the names of three convicted felons Bruno had arrested the previous year for burglary, a handful of others for petty crimes, a gang who'd robbed a bank, a woman who'd poisoned her husband with antifreeze, and a husband who'd killed his wife and kids with a gas leak.

Parker would check each of their whereabouts to see if one of them or a family member had threatened retribution after their arrest or incarceration.

According to Bruno's notes, the brother of the man convicted of killing his own family had insisted the man was innocent and had gotten violent after the sentencing.

Parker booted up his computer, accessed the police database, and discovered the man still lived in Savannah, and that he had been arrested for carrying a concealed weapon. A .38.

The same type of gun that had killed Bruno.

Surely Captain Black had investigated the man.

He phoned Bradford and asked. "Yeah, we questioned him," Bradford told him. "But he had an alibi for the night Bruno died. Why are you so interested?"

Good question. "His sister's my nurse," he admitted. "She asked me for help."

"The sister?"

"Yeah. I know she's talked to the captain, that she insists her brother didn't kill himself."

A long tense second stretched between them. "We all want the truth," Bradford finally said. "But I'm not sure we can trust everything Grace Gardener says."

Parker chewed the inside of his cheek. "Why not? She seems intelligent, sincere."

"You don't know about her past?"

"No." But his partner's tone jump-started his suspicions.

"Grace Gardener's father was a cop. At age seven, she saw her parents gunned down in front of her very eyes."

Oh, hell. "What about Bruno?"

"He was five, spending the night at a friend's house for a birthday party. Grace went into shock and had to undergo counseling."

"What are you saying? That Bruno's sister is not stable?"

Another pregnant pause. "That she might be in denial. A trauma like that affected both of them. I heard Bruno say that he felt guilty for not being home during the murder."

And that guilt could have driven the man to suicide.

"Did they find the parents' killer?"

"No," Bradford said. "But Bruno insisted he would."

"Maybe he did," Parker said. "And the killer murdered Bruno to silence him."

And if he did, and Grace kept nosing around, the guy might come after her, too.

GRACE TRIED DESPERATELY to regain control, but lost it as she tumbled down the cement steps. She screamed, throwing out her hands, her knees slicing painfully into the sharp concrete edge, but the dark inside of the stairwell blinded her and she couldn't see the rail. Whoever had pushed her had hit her with such force that she pitched headfirst, unable to stop until she reached the next landing, slamming into the wall.

She panted for a breath, her body trembling with shock as her muscles protested the awkward position, but she fought to rise to her knees.

She had to get up, run, escape…

But suddenly her attacker gripped her by the throat from behind. She tried to scream for help, but his fingers bit into her neck, cutting off her voice. Gasping, and struggling to pry his fingers away, she tried to remember the self-defense moves Bruno had shown her.

Lashing out, she brought one elbow up and slammed it backward into his chest, at the same time clawing at his hands. He grunted and momentarily loosened his hold. She swung backward again with her other elbow and knocked him down.

Her pulse racing, she pushed to her hands and knees, but a sharp pain splintered her ankle as she attempted to put weight on it and she nearly collapsed. Sheer determination drove her upward, though. He grunted and reached for her, but she lunged forward and stumbled down another step, pawing at the wall to guide her in the dark. The stench of stale air and sweat assailed her, making her break into a sprint. Another step. Another. She had to reach the next landing, make it into the hall…

Behind her, footsteps thudded ominously, making her chest pound with fear. Her ankle throbbed, and she hit the step edge and nearly fell, but managed to connect with the railing. Footsteps grew closer, and self-preservation took hold. She shoved the hair from her face and felt along the wall, heart racing as she stumbled to the door. Frantic, she pushed it open and fell into the corridor, tasting blood as she cried out for help.

The lights suddenly flickered on. She squinted, disoriented for a second as her eyes adjusted to the light. The hall was empty, and she jumped up and barreled around the corner. When she spotted the nurses' station, she dived toward it.

"Help me!"

Doris, one of the head nurses on the second floor, jerked her head up. "Grace?"

She staggered toward the desk. "Someone attacked me in the stairwell. Call security!"

Doris's eyes widened in shock, but she immediately catapulted into motion and punched the security alarm. Grace leaned against the desk, trembling and trying to steady her breathing.

Doris raced around the edge of the station. "My God, Grace, are you all right?"

She nodded and wiped blood from her lip with the back of her hand.

Doris slid an arm around Grace's waist. "Come on, honey, you need to sit down. I'll get a doctor."

Grace nodded, and Doris helped her to a chair behind the desk, then called one of the ER physicians.

A security guard rushed up. "What's going on?"

Doris gestured toward Grace. "Someone attacked Grace in the stairwell."

"He pushed me down the steps," Grace said.

The guard flipped on his radio and reported the attack. "Secure and check all stairwells." He turned to Grace. "Did you get a look at your attacker?"

She shook her head no. "The lights went out and it was so dark I couldn't see anything."

The guard gave a clipped nod, then turned and moved to the stairwell. He removed his gun and inched inside, then disappeared down the steps.

The next few minutes passed in a blur for Grace as Dr. Stoddard, one of the residents in ER, escorted her to an exam room. He examined her, took her vitals and cleaned her knees and hands.

Dr. Whitehead strode in, looking worried and agitated. "Good God, Grace. I just heard. What happened?"

She was still shaking, and hated the quiver to her voice but couldn't control it as she relayed the details of the attack.

Who would hurt her? And why would someone try to kill her? Because she'd been asking questions about the tissue transplants? Because she'd been pushing the cops to investigate Bruno's death?

Or because she'd possibly seen a murderer in the graveyard the night before?

PARKER WANTED TO TALK to Grace. Find out more about her parents' murder.

But would she want to discuss it with him? Had Bruno discovered some new evidence that had gotten him killed?

He accessed the police department files and skimmed the details of that crime. Mr. and Mrs. Jim Gardener had been murdered in their home one night around midnight. Their seven-year-old daughter had witnessed the brutal shooting.

The crime photos depicted the bloody gore in vivid clarity. Blood and brain matter had splattered all over their bodies, the sofa and walls.

Grace had seen it all….

His stomach knotted, but he read on.

According to the papers, after the attack, she'd been terrified the killer would find her so she'd hidden in the attic inside a trunk filled with old clothing. She'd stayed there for hours, until morning, terrified and shivering. She'd fallen asleep, had awakened certain she'd had a terrible nightmare. But when she'd tiptoed down the stairs and looked into the den, her parents had been lying in a pool of blood and she started screaming....

He imagined Grace as a small child, innocent, sweet, trusting—her world shattered by the vicious slaying of her parents. How did a child survive an ordeal like that and be normal? How had she grown into such a caring person, nursing and taking care of others, when she'd lost so much to violence at such a young age?

He zoned in on the facts of the crime.

The Gardeners had been shot at close range in the head by a .38 automatic—the same type of gun that had killed their son. The similarity raised a red flag. Coincidence or not?

He didn't like coincidences.

Unless Bruno's killer wanted the cops to think that the same person was responsible, to throw them off track.

He fished through all the information he could find on the arrest in the Gardener case and realized that the police had never found any substantial leads….

No wonder Grace didn't want the same thing to happen to her brother.

Had he been murdered, instead of taking his own life?

A commotion in the hall made him jerk his head up, and he put his computer aside, climbed from bed, then walked to the doorway. When he opened it, he saw two security guards rushing down the hall. Several nurses hovered in the central nurses' station visible from his door.

What in the hell was going on?

A bad premonition twisted his insides and he hobbled to the knot of nurses, their hushed whispers and agitated expressions alarming him more. He searched the faces for Grace, but didn't see her.

One of the RNs noticed him and frowned, her thick eyebrows pinching together. "Mr. Kilpatrick, all the patients need to stay in their rooms right now."

He straightened. "What's going on?"

"One of our nurses was attacked, and the security guards are searching the building." She took his arm. "Please, they asked us to keep all patients out of the hallways until they've swept the facility."

His heart pounded but he didn't budge. "Who was attacked?"

She shot the other nurses a frantic look as if to call in reinforcements. "Grace Gardener."

He sucked in a sharp breath. "Is she all right?"

A young nurse's assistant closed the distance between them. "They took her to the ER. Someone tried to choke her."

Parker's blood ran cold. He headed to the elevator but the RN grabbed his arm. "Please, Mr. Kilpatrick—"

"Detective," he barked as he glared down at her. "And you're not going to stop me, miss. I'm going to see Grace right now, so step aside. This is a police investigation."

She bristled, her shocked look turning to anger at his tactics. But he didn't give a damn. He had to make sure Grace was all right.

Then he'd find out who in hell had assaulted her and shove his fist down the bastard's throat.

Chapter Six

Time stalled for Parker as he hobbled to the ER. He had to see for himself that she was all right.

He spotted several security guards checking the halls and staircases. But there were so many places to hide….

His leg stiffened as he stopped at the nurses' desk, but he ignored the throbbing pain. "Which room is Grace Gardener in?"

The gray-haired woman pursed her lips. "You're a patient?"

"Yes, but I'm also a police detective. Parker Kilpatrick." He straightened to his full six-two, wishing he was in street clothes, not his T-shirt and sweatpants. "I heard there was an incident."

"Yes, poor thing is in Exam Room Three. Dr. Stoddard and Dr. Whitehead are examining her now."

"Which way?"

Her face flashed with confusion. "You should go back to your room. I'm sure an officer is on his way."

"I'm here," he said brusquely. "And I'm going to see Grace."

Her eyes narrowed at his commanding tone, but she rose, guided him through a corridor and knocked on the door, then stuck her head in. "Dr. Whitehead, Dr. Stoddard, there's a police detective here."

"Send him in," Dr. Whitehead said.

The nurse stepped aside and Parker shuffled in, his heartbeat racing when he spotted Grace on the exam table.

Scrapes and abrasions marred her knees and hands, and a bruise colored her forehead. He balled his hands into fists as he zeroed in on the outline of the man's fingers forming on her neck.

He clenched his jaw in a futile attempt to tame his temper. "Grace, are you all right?"

Her eyes looked luminous with tears and fear strained her features, but she nodded.

Dr. Whitehead stood way too close, one hand on Grace's shoulder as if he'd been soothing her. For some reason, the sight of the man beside Grace irritated Parker more.

The doctor's lips thinned. "Detective Kilpatrick, I called the police to report the incident, but I wasn't expecting you. You're a patient."

Parker cleared his throat. "The department will send someone over. Now tell me what happened."

The young resident stood where he'd been putting antiseptic on Grace's knee and aimed a smile at Parker. "She's going to be fine. Minor cuts and abrasions."

Parker didn't return the smile. "Except that someone obviously tried to strangle her."

Grace's chin quivered and she twisted her fingers together and stared at them. Two of her nails were broken, meaning she must have torn them during the attack.

"You scratched your attacker?"

"Yes," she said softly.

"Good." Parker leveled his tone, knowing he'd sounded brusque and unfeeling. But he had a job to do, and it was taking all his restraint not to move forward and touch Grace, to hold her and make sure she was okay, for himself.

"We'll take samples," he said, "and we'll need to try to see if we can lift a print from your neck. It's hard to get one from skin but we might get a partial."

She nodded silently, and another knock sounded at the door.

"This is Grand Central Station," Dr. Whitehead snarled as he opened the door and a uniformed officer from the S.P.D. entered and introduced himself. Parker recognized him, a twenty-something recruit named Owens who was still green around the collar.

"Someone called in an assault?" Owens asked.

Parker filled him in. "Yes. Miss Gardener was accosted. We need to try to get fingerprints, and scrape beneath her nails."

Dr. Whitehead stroked Grace's back. "Grace, I have a surgery scheduled. If you're all right—"

"I'm fine, please go back to work, Doctor."

Parker gritted his teeth. He didn't like the man touching her.

Dr. Whitehead gave him an odd look, then excused himself. Officer Owens came back in with a kit and began to take samples from beneath Grace's fingernails.

Parker took the lead in questioning her. "Grace, can you tell us exactly what happened?"

She nodded again, but her voice wobbled when she spoke. "I was going down the stairs—"

He cut in. "Why did you choose the stairs, and not the elevator?"

She bit down on her lower lip. "It was storming and the lights flicked off once, so I was nervous about getting in the elevator. I…I'm claustrophobic."

He swallowed hard. Probably from being trapped in that trunk when she was little. "Go on."

"Anyway, when I was inside, the lights went off again, and I tried to feel my way down, then I heard footsteps…" Her voice broke, and she inhaled shakily. "Then someone pushed me from behind. I tried to fight him but lost my balance and tumbled down to the landing."

He wanted to kill the guy and put his arms around her at the same time, but he forced himself to remain in place.

Her eyes teared up, but she wiped them away with a scraped hand. "Then he came at me on the landing…that's when he tried to strangle me."

He fisted his hands to keep from reaching for her. "Did you see him? Can you tell me anything about him?"

"No. It was so dark I couldn't see."

"Did he say anything?"

She shook her head. "No, I just heard him breathing. And he smelled like sweat…"

He sighed. Not much to go on. But if she'd gotten some skin beneath her fingernails, they might get some DNA.

GRACE HATED all the attention.

Flashbacks of her childhood, of police,

reporters, concerned neighbors and friends of her family coming to call, rose to taunt her. She'd tried to be tough back then, but for years afterward she'd been self-conscious. Had felt as if she'd been placed under a microscope like a bug and dissected by professionals for the world to see.

Everyone had wanted to know about the little girl who'd witnessed her parents' brutal murder.

What had she seen? Would she remember more details as she grew older? Was she stable?

Would the killer come after her?

The hushed whispers taunted her. She appeared to be all right. Was a strong little girl. Would she have a breakdown sometime later in life? Sometimes children who'd experienced severe trauma turned out to be psychotic. Suicidal. Unable to cope. Suffered from depression. Alcoholism.

Even multiple personality disorder.

The fringes of depression had plucked at her at times, the nightmares tormenting her.

But she'd always fought her way back. She would now, too. She wouldn't let this incident, this attack, shake the foundation she'd so carefully carved for herself.

She met Parker's gaze. He was watching her with the strangest look in his eyes. Almost like Bruno had when he'd launched into brotherly, protective, male-macho mode.

Except Parker's look didn't appear brotherly. For a moment when he'd first come in and their eyes had locked, she'd felt a bolt of something sexual. An awareness on a level that she hadn't felt for a man in a long time.

Maybe ever.

Dr. Whitehead had also been concerned but she'd shrunk from his touch. Hadn't felt comforted but uncomfortable.

But with Parker…

Good grief. What in the world was happening to her? She was fantasizing about an attraction with the detective when she was bruised and harried-looking, trembling from fear and torn between screaming her outrage at the man who'd shoved her down the stairs and running into Parker's big, safe arms.

He would think she was crazy if she threw herself at him.

The officer from the police department finished taking notes on her statement just as a security guard appeared. "Stanley Mervin," the guard said in introduction. "We didn't find anyone in the staircase."

"You have cameras in the stairwells?" Parker asked.

The guard shifted and looked down at his scuffed-up shoes. "No. I guess we should install them."

A moment of guilt tugged at Grace. Parker shouldn't be dealing with her problems when he was recovering from surgery.

"Parker, I'm fine. Why don't you go back and rest? I'm sure this officer can handle things now."

"Grace. I can do my job." He shot her a cold look.

Like her father and brother, Parker thrived on the job. Obviously she'd insulted him by pointing out his physical weakness. She wanted to apologize but emphasizing her role as his nurse might make matters worse. Especially in front of the other cop.

"We'll review the tapes of the halls and corridors for someone suspicious exiting the stairwells," the security guard offered.

"Yes, do that," Parker growled. "I want to see them, too."

"I'll go set it up." The guard left with a clipped nod, and she and Parker were alone.

His heavy sigh rattled between them. "Damn it, Grace, are you really okay?"

She nodded, moisture burning her eyelids at the concern in his voice.

He leaned closer, within an inch of her face. She closed her eyes, ached for him to hold her, to kiss her, but his fingers traced a line over the bruises on her neck.

"Do you have any idea who the guy was?"

She shook her head no and opened her eyes to see him staring at her. He was so near she could see the fine bristles of his beard stubble where he needed to shave.

She inhaled the hospital soap on his skin, felt his breath on her face.

She must be desperate and delusional, but she wanted him to kiss her.

"Let's review the time line of events before the attack," he said, oblivious to her thoughts. "What were you doing?"

A knot twisted her stomach. "You mean, after I saw you?"

His eyes darkened as if he suddenly remembered their conversation over coffee. The fact that she'd been asking about the tissue transplants, talking about her brother.

"Grace?"

She studied her broken nails. Inanely thought how much she needed a manicure. How she liked to keep lotion on her hands to make them soft so when she tended to the patients her skin wasn't abrasive.

On the heels of those thoughts, helplessness set in.

"Grace?"

She sucked in a breath. "I was on my way to the records department to look at Bruno's autopsy report."

A long silence fell between them, fraught with tension. "Did you tell anyone what you were going to do?"

She shook her head.

But what if someone had overheard their conversation? What if someone hadn't wanted her to see Bruno's autopsy report?

PARKER HATED putting the fear back in Grace's eyes, but she couldn't snoop around on her own. For God's sake, she'd almost been killed.

And as much as he wanted to protect her, he wasn't exactly in top shape.

"Grace, I want to look at those security tapes. Are you going to stay here?"

She glanced around the small exam room. "No, I'll go with you. If there's something on the tape, I want to see it."

"That's probably a good idea," he agreed. "You can identify staff members and point out if someone looks out of place."

Because whoever had attacked her could easily have been a staff member or worn a disguise. He could have dressed like one of the cleaning staff, a cook, a doctor or other medical personnel and slipped through the halls without even being noticed.

What if her attacker was someone she knew?

"DAMN IT, the bitch got away."

"You fool, why did you attack her in the hospital?"

His voice echoed low and menacing. "Because she's asking too many questions."

He twisted the phone cord in his hand, contemplating how to handle the situation. So far, he'd covered his tracks. And now with the corpses cropping up all over town… "Relax. She doesn't know anything."

"She's friendly with that cop." His breathing sounded choppy in the strained silence. "I heard them talking about her brother's death. She sounded suspicious."

"That doesn't mean she'll find any answers. They can't link Bruno's death to us." He wheezed a breath. "Think about it—another dead body would only make the cops take another look at his case."

"They never give up on cop killers," he growled.

He was right. Maybe the attack today had scared Grace off nosing around, though. But if she did keep digging and linked Bruno's death to him, then he'd make sure she ended up six feet under, just like Bruno.

Chapter Seven

Parker itched to put his arm around Grace and support her as they left the ER, but he was walking a fine line—technically, Officer Owens was in charge, but the young cop screamed rookie, and he might miss something.

Grace's safety was too important for Parker to rely on anyone but himself.

The security guard led them to an office that housed monitors for all the security cameras throughout the building. The guard watching the monitors, a sixty-year-old gray-haired man with bifocals and a nasally voice that hinted at sleep apnea, introduced himself as Leon Banks.

"I'm Detective Kilpatrick and this is Officer Owens," Parker said. "This is

Grace Gardener, the woman who was accosted in the stairwell earlier."

The older man scratched his craggy chin. "I heard about it. Sorry I didn't see anything."

Parker grimaced. The old coot had probably nodded off. "We need to check the monitors," he said. "Our unknown subject, UNSUB, was in the stairwell. He had to get in and out of the hospital some way without drawing suspicion." He glanced at Grace and saw her grappling for control. He'd seen plenty of witnesses fall apart after an assault, but she had kept her cool. She was gutsy, strong, smart.

And so damned beautiful, she stole his breath.

How could any man use physical force against a woman, especially her? Grace was a healer, and the most giving woman he'd ever met.

Which meant he had to find out the identity of the man who'd tried to kill her and make him pay. But he lowered his voice, hoping to soothe her. "Grace, approximately what time did the attack occur?"

"Around five. It was only minutes after I left you."

Parker gestured toward the cameras. "Let's check all the feeds an hour prior to that, especially ones near the elevators, doors and stairwells. We'll move from there through the time of the attack and the following half hour. He wouldn't have stuck around long after that."

Banks twisted his mouth sideways in skepticism. "Sounds like a plan."

Parker barely resisted a curse. He'd thought the hospital was better equipped than this. Had budgets run low or was the facility simply not accustomed to crime?

GRACE STUDIED the tapes, her eyes darting from one camera to the next. Parker, Officer Owens and the security guard were all focused on examining the shots, as well.

Unfortunately nothing jumped out at them. But the dark shadows of the hallway and corridors reminded her of the cold reality of the assault.

She leaned forward, desperately searching for some sign that would reveal the identity of her attacker.

Had the man left the hospital after she'd fallen? Or had he hidden out somewhere inside? He could have disappeared into a lab, a janitor's closet, a patient's room, the cafeteria, the morgue....

And what if he wasn't an outsider but one of the staff? She'd headed toward records. What if someone had overheard and didn't want her to see Bruno's autopsy? Or what if someone didn't like her asking questions about the tissue transplants?

Maybe the lab technician or doctor who'd contaminated the tissue was worried about getting caught.

One segment suddenly caught her eye. A man wearing surgical scrubs with his face averted from the camera. His body language, scrunched shoulders and shrunken posture suggested that he was hiding something. Not as confident as most of the doctors she knew.

And then there was another man in a work uniform. He, too, had his face angled away from the camera, hat pulled low on his forehead. And he was wearing work gloves.

"Can you freeze that section, then isolate the man in scrubs, then the one in the uniform?" Parker asked, as if he, too, noticed the same suspicious behavior.

The security guard shrugged, but complied. Grace narrowed her eyes, trying to discern the man's face, any features or distinguishing marks, but the camera shot seemed out of focus and she couldn't make out the doctor's face.

The same was true with the man in the uniform. He had hidden himself well.

Parker pointed to the man in scrubs. "Ask one of your team to freeze-frame this and show it around the hospital. I want to know if this man is on staff."

The guard nodded, and Parker leaned closer, studying the other man more closely. "The hat indicates he's from a work crew. Either that or he stole the uniform as a cover." Parker cleared his throat. "It looks like there's an emblem for a painting company on the pocket.

Maybe if we isolate that and enlarge it, we can track down the company. See if they sent a worker out here on a job, and cross-reference it with official work orders from the hospital."

Although hope budded in Grace's chest that this was her attacker, she also realized that they were searching for a needle in a haystack. "Or he could just be a visitor here to see a friend or family member."

Parker gave her an encouraging look. "Maybe. But I'm going to send these tapes to our team and see what they can come up with. Maybe they can bring the photo into focus and we can ID this guy."

Grace's heart raced. "You think he's the man who attacked me?"

Questions and anger darkened his eyes. "I don't know. But if he is, we'll nail him, Grace."

She wanted to believe him, to trust that he meant every word that he said. That for once the justice system would work. But she'd been alone a long time, had been disappointed time and time again.

And as much as she wanted this photograph to lead them to her assailant, fear clogged her throat.

She hadn't felt safe since her parents had been murdered. Hadn't trusted anyone but Bruno and now he was dead.

She didn't know if she could trust anyone now, or if she'd ever truly feel safe again.

PARKER DIDN'T KNOW if the man on camera was the perp, but he had to pursue the tape as a possible lead.

Unless Grace had DNA beneath her fingernails—then they could nail the bastard.

Until then he had to convince Grace to lie low.

Officer Owens confiscated the tapes and left to take them to the crime lab while Parker and Grace headed back to his room. Thank God his leg was healing and he felt stronger, or maybe he was just pumped with adrenaline from finally getting back to work.

And from knowing that he had to protect Grace.

He didn't have time to convalesce.

Although the captain would never agree to let him come back officially, not yet.

When they reached his room, Grace turned to him. She looked pale and shaken, and so vulnerable with the bruises darkening her neck and forehead that his gut tightened.

"Parker, thank you for going with me to view those tapes."

"You don't have to thank me, Grace. I was doing my job."

"You're not on duty, you're a patient—"

He silenced her with a glare. "My mind isn't damaged," he said sharply. "I'm still competent, Grace, and I'm improving every day."

"I know, Parker, and I'm not trying to insult you." Her voice softened, ripping at his gut. "What I meant was that I really appreciated you being there."

He hesitated, unable to keep from touching her another second. Her eyes were the most luminous shade of blue he'd ever seen, angel eyes. Her lips the color of raspberries. Her skin like cream.

Someone had almost strangled her earlier, and if he'd succeeded, Parker would have never known how it felt to hold her.

Her breath quickened as he gently tucked an errant strand of hair behind her ear. The movement revealed the length of the bruises on her neck, stirring his anger and…his need.

Unable to stand it a moment longer, he pressed his hand against her cheek. Grace deserved tenderness, love.

Which he couldn't give her.

The thought sobered him and he started to pull away, but she leaned into his hand and closed her eyes as if she needed him. His resistance disintegrated and he pulled her into his arms.

For a moment she seemed hesitant, but finally she relaxed and rested against his chest. He was a foot taller than Grace, but she fit perfectly into his arms, and he lowered his head against hers and stroked her back. Her whispered sign of acceptance aroused every protective bone in his body.

"It's going to be all right," he said into her hair.

"I was so scared, Parker."

He smiled at her confession. "I know."

Her body shuddered and he cradled her tighter. "I promise you I'll find out who tried to hurt you."

She nodded and curled her fingers into his back, and his body surged to life with desire.

A desire he couldn't follow through on.

"Kilpatrick?"

Parker stiffened at the sound of his partner's voice, and pulled away from Grace. Damn. A flush of embarrassment colored her cheeks and she fussed with her hair. The gesture was so utterly female that he almost smiled again, but Bradford was watching him with his dark eyebrows drawn.

"I heard someone was attacked here," Bradford said.

Parker nodded. "Yes, someone tried to push Grace down the stairs."

Bradford's gaze instantly shot to Grace, and like a seasoned detective, he zoned in on the bruises on her neck and face. "Did you see the guy?"

She shook her head no. Parker's leg ached, so he walked over and sat on the bed to alleviate the pressure. Grace claimed the chair while Bradford stood by the bed, angling himself so he could watch both of them.

"We just came from studying the security camera tapes," Parker said. "Owens is carrying them to the lab to have our guys examine them. We have a couple of images that need to be enhanced."

"Good. Anything else?"

"It's possible that Grace scratched her attacker so we might have some DNA."

"Excellent." Bradford shifted sideways. "Any description?"

"I'm afraid not," Grace said, then explained about the power outage.

Outside, the storm had settled down, although dark clouds still hung low, turning the sky a dismal gray.

"Miss Gardener—"

She cut him off. "Please call me Grace."

"Grace, can you think of anyone who'd want to hurt you?" Bradford asked.

She twisted her hands together, then stared at them as if they might offer answers. "No."

"Do you have any enemies?" Bradford asked.

She shook her head, looking startled at the question. "Not anyone that I know of."

Anticipating Bradford's next question, Parker decided to ask it first. "What about a boyfriend or lover?"

Her wide-eyed gaze swung to his, and he realized he should have allowed Bradford to voice the question. She obviously thought it personal.

Which made him more curious about the answer.

He'd been thinking all along that her snooping into Bruno's death had brought an attacker to her door, but what if it was as simple as the fact that she had an ex-boyfriend or lover she'd recently broken up with? One who wanted her back?

One so obsessed that he'd do anything, even kill her, to keep her from being with another man?

GRACE STARED at Parker, momentarily stunned by his question. Why was he asking about her prior relationships?

She'd felt the hum of attraction mounting inside of her when he'd held her, but had assumed that it had been one-sided. As a cop, he probably had terrified women falling into his arms on a daily basis.

Heck, he was so darned handsome that a woman didn't have to be terrified to want his arms around her.

What was she thinking?

Parker was not only a patient, but a cop. The last person in the world she should pursue a relationship with.

And why did he want to know about the men she'd been involved with? Was his question personal or professional?

"Grace?" Parker's voice resonated louder this time, as if tinged with impatience.

"What does my personal life have to do with today's attack?"

"That's what we're trying to figure out,"

Parker said. "One possibility is that the assault on you was random. Another is that a former boyfriend or lover might be stalking you. Although in light of the fact that you might have seen a murderer the other night at the graveyard, and that you've been pushing the police to investigate your brother's death, it's doubtful."

A cold chill slithered through her.

"I'm sorry, Grace," Parker said, "but we have to consider the fact that this perp targeted you specifically, meaning he had a motive. That means we need to consider every angle."

So Parker wasn't interested personally. Her skin crawled with humiliation for allowing her imagination to stray.

"It may lead to nothing," Bradford interjected. "But at least we can eliminate any past boyfriends as suspects."

She hated to divulge the fact that she hadn't had anyone special in her life in a long time. Not since college and that relationship had ended disastrously. She'd woken in the throes of a nightmare one too many times, and the guy had walked out, saying she was crazy. "There's no one," she admitted.

Parker's gaze seemed glued to hers. "How about someone you dated casually? Maybe someone who wanted to take it a step further but you declined?"

"There is no one," she said, although Dr. Whitehead's interest in her teased the back of her mind. But he was a renowned surgeon. Half the nurses at the hospital swooned over him. He certainly wasn't obsessed with her, or dangerous.

"No, I can't think of anyone," she said quietly.

"What were you doing before the attack?" Bradford asked.

She glanced at Parker to ask if she should confide her suspicions and he nodded. "All these missing bodies…it made me remember that my brother's body went missing for two days after he was sent to the morgue. I started thinking about reasons someone would steal a corpse, and wanted to look at Bruno's autopsy and the exam report after his body was recovered."

"A copy of his autopsy report along

with that other one should be in his file," Bradford said.

Parker nodded and reached for the file Bradford had dropped off earlier, the one he had yet to look at.

He flipped it open and searched inside, his gut churning. "I hate to tell you this, but both reports are missing."

Chapter Eight

"Why would someone take the report?" Grace asked.

Parker tempered his irritation. "I don't know, but we'll request another copy. Did Bruno say anything to you about your parents' case? Had he found a new clue?"

Tension strained Grace's features. "No, not that I remember."

Dr. Whitehead poked his head into the room. "There you are, Grace. I thought I might find you here."

She jerked her head toward him and Parker grimaced. She might not be involved with Whitehead, but the man was definitely interested in her.

"This is Detective Walsh." Grace stood to introduce the two men.

Dr. Whitehead's smile seemed tight. Then again, if he cared for Grace, he was probably simply concerned.

"Did you find anything on the tapes?" Dr. Whitehead asked.

Parker explained about the shadowed face and that they'd check for DNA under Grace's fingernails, then Whitehead turned to Grace. "You look exhausted. Why don't I give you a lift home?"

She bit down on her lip. "I was getting ready to go, but I have my car."

"You can leave it here tonight and pick it up tomorrow. I don't think you should drive yourself, Grace."

"I'm fine," Grace said. "I don't want to be any trouble."

"No trouble, but if you insist on driving, I'll follow you home and make sure you get in safely."

She bit her lip. She claimed she wasn't involved with anyone. Had she lied?

Did she care what he thought?

Damn it, he wished he could drive her home and check her house. Make sure no one was waiting inside.

Make certain that Whitehead didn't get too close to her.

"That would be nice," she said, but paused. "Parker, Detective Walsh, please let me know what you find out."

Both men nodded, then she walked out the door with Whitehead. Parker fought back a snarl.

"What's going on with you and Grace Gardener?" Bradford asked.

Parker cut him a scathing look. "Nothing."

"It sure as hell looked like something."

"Don't go there, man. She was shaken up after the attack, and I tried to comfort her. That's all."

"Right. And that bear look on your face when Whitehead offered to take her home?"

Parker grimaced. Had he really been that transparent? "It's nothing personal. I just think he's too smooth."

"And too interested in Grace?"

"Look, Walsh, she's in danger. Like you said. We have to look at everyone as a suspect."

Walsh chuckled, annoying Parker even more, but he let it drop. "Let's see if we can obtain another copy of that medical report on Bruno."

Bradford nodded. "I'll get right on it."

"Meanwhile I'll continue looking at Bruno's cases. Maybe he found a lead on his parents' murder and that got him killed."

"Okay, start sifting through the old files." Bradford's cell phone rang and he snapped it open. "Walsh." A pause. "All right. I'll be right there."

He frowned as he closed the phone. "I have to go. Another decimated body was just found."

"Where?"

"On the doorstep of an old church on Tybee Island."

Parker's throat convulsed. He didn't like the sound of that.

Grace had told him that she lived on Tybee.

GRACE SHIVERED as she passed the grave-yard on Tybee. Two police cars with blue lights twirling sat like guards to the entrance, another one in front of the small church.

What had happened? Had a crime occurred at the church? Had a grave been vandalized or robbed? Or had another missing body turned up here?

The stories of ghosts haunting the island echoed in her head, raising her anxiety, and as she glanced at the trees lining the road, a ghostly figure floated in and out of the darkness.

She checked her rearview mirror and saw Wilson Whitehead's headlights behind her, and felt a small measure of comfort that he was following her home. Although she didn't want him to come in and stay….

Five minutes later she turned into her drive and parked, climbed out, then raked her hair back from her forehead as a warm breeze tossed it across her face. The sound of Wilson's car door slamming cut into the roar of the ocean in the distance. His shoes crunched on the clam-shelled drive as he walked toward her.

"I made it fine," she said. "Thanks for following me home."

"I'm going to check the inside of your cottage," he said.

His comment reminded her that earlier someone had tried to kill her. "Thanks."

He gave a clipped nod, followed her to the small front porch and waited as she unlocked the door. She flipped on the light in the small foyer, casting a soft glow across the worn furnishings and oak floor. The house seemed quiet, only the soft rattle of the wind hitting the windows breaking the silence. He quickly checked the rooms while she moved to the kitchen to make some coffee. A noise startled her and she inched to the laundry room and opened the door, then frowned.

The curtain flapped against the window, and the window was open. Had she left it that way or had an intruder opened it and come in?

"Everything looks fine." Wilson's voice startled her and she spun around. "Grace, are you all right?"

A nervous laugh escaped her. "Yes, I'm sorry. Just jumpy."

He stroked her arm. "I'd be glad to stay with you tonight."

She locked the window, then turned back to him. "No, thanks, Wilson. I appreciate the offer but I'm a big girl. I'll be fine."

"I really don't mind," he said with a smile. "We could be good together, Grace."

Her chest squeezed. "Wilson, please… this isn't a good time."

Disappointment flattened his eyes, but he nodded. "I know you've had a rough day. I could make us some dinner."

She shook her head. "I really am tired. I just want a hot bath and to go to bed."

"All right. But you have my number."

She nodded, then walked him to the door. "Thanks again. I'll see you at the hospital tomorrow."

"Call me if you need anything, Grace. Any time, day or night."

She thanked him again, then twisted the lock behind him. Her muscles ached from her tumble down the steps, so she ran a hot bath, poured bath salts in, then grabbed a glass of wine to sip while she soaked her battered body. The warm, soapy bubbles felt heavenly, and she closed her eyes, forcing memories of the attack at bay.

Wilson's face flashed into her mind, his offer to stay reverberating in her head. He was handsome, intelligent, a doctor. And he was interested in her. So why wasn't she attracted to him?

Another man's face flashed in her mind instead. Parker's. For a moment she imagined him staying with her tonight, offering her comfort, protecting her.

Holding her. Touching her. Making love to her.

A sound outside jarred her back to reality and she opened her eyes, knotting her hands in frustration. Why was she thinking of Parker Kilpatrick, a detective who had the power to break her heart?

A cop who might not even be attracted to her….

Her telephone jangled. She grabbed a towel, patted dry, then wrapped it around her and hurried to answer the phone, half hoping it was Parker. Instead the Caller ID showed Frank Johnson. He had been her father's partner, and an uncle of sorts to her and Bruno after her parents had been murdered. She knew he'd felt guilty about not being able to solve the crime. What did he want now? Could he possibly have news about the decades-old murders or about Bruno's?

The ringing continued and she answered it. "Hello, Frank."

"Jesus, Grace, I was beginning to think you wouldn't answer. I've been worried out of my mind tonight."

"Sorry, I was in the bath."

"Are you okay? I heard that you were attacked at the hospital today."

Agitation tinged his voice, and guilt assailed her. He had enough on his plate with his ill daughter. "I'm fine," she said, although her hand automatically touched the bruises on her neck. "I just fell down the steps."

"You were attacked?"

She sighed. "Yes, someone pushed me from behind."

"And you filed a report?"

"Yes."

"Did you get a look at your attacker?"

Even though he was retired, he still sounded like a cop. "No, Frank. The power flickered off, and it was so dark I couldn't see. But I think I scratched him. And don't worry, the police processed me for evidence."

His labored breathing rattled over the line. "Good. Do you want to stay with me and Kelly tonight?"

She smiled at his fatherly tone. "Thanks, Frank, but I'm fine here, really. The doors are locked and I have my cell phone if I need to call for help."

"I just don't want anything to happen to you." His voice broke. "It was bad enough losing Bruno…."

Ever since her parents' death, Frank had thought of Bruno as a son, and it had hit him hard when he'd died, especially when the cops had called his death a suicide. Frank blamed himself for not being able to help Bruno. But he had accepted the suicide theory more readily than she had,

had admitted that he'd known Bruno was depressed, that he suspected he'd been drinking too much. That he understood because he'd experienced similar feelings after their father's death.

"How's Kelly?" she asked, hoping to divert his attention away from her.

The long pause reverberated with tension. "She's not doing so well. She's had some kind of viral infection that won't go away. I…it doesn't look good."

Her heart swelled with a dull ache. Kelly had cerebral palsy and her health had declined drastically the past five years. She didn't know how Frank would handle it if he lost his only child. Her mother had died long ago.

"I'll try to drop by and see her soon. You take care of her and yourself."

"I will. But, Grace, call me if you need anything. I may be retired, but I can call in a favor if you need protection."

Parker Kilpatrick's face flashed in Grace's mind and she bit her lip to keep from mentioning him, then thanked Frank and hung up.

A sudden noise jerked her head toward the window and she froze, wondering if someone was out back.

Her hand trembled as she shifted the edge of the curtain aside, then she peered through the glass pane into the darkness. The palm trees swayed with the breeze, the sound of the ocean roar mingling with its shrill whistle. Maybe the wind had simply tossed a garbage can lid across the shells or blown something over. But a slight movement caught her eye and she tensed.

Was she imagining things or had someone been by her car?

PARKER WAS STRUNG so tight he couldn't sleep. He kept imagining Grace at home alone with a killer stalking her. Kept seeing her falling down those steps, screaming for help, a man's hands gripping her throat and strangling her.

Damn it, he hated knowing that he was in the hospital while she might need him.

Determined to get to the bottom of her brother's death, he checked Bruno's files

again but found no details on his investi-
gations.

The missing autopsy report disturbed
him. If someone had stolen it, perhaps
they'd also stolen information from his
police files.

But the police were the only ones with
access to that data.

He punched in Bradford's number, then
remembered that he'd gone to Tybee
because of another body. "It's Kilpatrick.
What'd do you find at the church on
Tybee?"

"Female corpse. No ID yet."

"What was the state of the corpse?"

"Face was heavily made-up like the
others and signs indicate she was autop-
sied. We're still photographing the
scene, collecting forensics. We won't
know more until after the ME gets her on
the table."

"Let me know. And tell them to check
and see if she had any tissues or organs
removed."

"What? You think these pranks are a
cover-up for a more sinister motive?"

"Maybe. It's worth exploring," Parker said.

Bradford hesitated. "I'll get copies of reports on all the bodies we've recovered so far and bring them over. While I'm out chasing leads and talking to the victims' families and friends, maybe you can search for a pattern."

Parker pulled a hand down his face in relief. Finally, Walsh was treating him like a partner again, not an invalid. "Did you request another autopsy report on Bruno?"

"Yeah, and you won't believe it, but the medical examiner's copy is missing, as well."

"How about the computer file?"

"Deleted."

Parker cursed. "Can we get a warrant for our tech team to try to retrieve it?"

Bradford hesitated. "I'll take care of it."

Parker flexed his leg, stretching the muscles as his physical therapist recommended. "Good. I think someone is after Grace because of Bruno's death or because he'd discovered new clues about his parents' murder."

"Sounds feasible," Bradford admitted. "So what do you need?"

"I want to talk to Bruno's partner. What do you know about the guy?"

"His name is David Roundtree. He's been on the force for a couple of years. Not married. Transferred from somewhere up north."

"He have a past?"

"I don't know. You want me to look into it?"

"Yeah."

"Parker, I know you want to help this nurse, but—"

"Don't give me any lectures, Walsh. I feel better tonight than I have in months. Besides, you guys have to be swamped with the body snatcher cases."

A long pause. "Right. Listen, I have to get back to the crime scene here. I'll drop those files off in the morning."

"Thanks." Parker hung up, then phoned the medical examiner, but he wasn't in. "Who is this?"

"The assistant medical examiner, Lamar Poultry."

Parker identified himself. "Poultry, we're looking for information about Bruno Gardener. Did you autopsy him?"

"I assisted."

"How about when his body went missing and was recovered?"

"That was a clerical error," Poultry said. "But we did examine him and didn't find anything unusual."

Parker grimaced. Grace would be grateful to hear that, but he still wanted to see the reports. He decided not to tell Poultry about the warrant, so he thanked him and hung up, then paced across the room. He had a knot in the pit of his stomach that wouldn't go away. Grace had survived the attack tonight. But his gut instincts told him that the guy would return for her.

Parker didn't want her to be alone when he did.

GRACE STARED THROUGH the window, searching the woods until her eyes ached from the strain. A dog barked in the distance and she spotted a deer suddenly shoot from the edge of the trees near her car.

A breath of relief whisked out and she finally relaxed, chiding herself for being paranoid.

Yet someone had tried to kill her, and who knew if they'd try again? Maybe he was watching her now....

She gripped her hands into fists. She might have lost everyone she'd ever loved, but she refused to become a prisoner of fear. Then he would destroy her, too. And she was going to beat this guy, find out who he was, if he'd killed Bruno and her parents.

If he had, she wanted him to pay.

Still, she wasn't a fool. Looking into both cases had put her in danger. And it had cost Bruno his life. She had to be smart. Careful.

Her mind turned back to Parker Kilpatrick again and relief swelled inside her—just knowing that he was helping her gave her confidence. Taking thoughts of him with her, she finally crawled into bed and tried to sleep.

Unfortunately, instead of a peaceful sleep, her dreams were filled with murder and death.

BRUNO HAD DIED with his secrets.

And if Grace Gardener kept pushing, she would die, too.

She was asking too many questions. Talking to that cop Kilpatrick.

He had to stop her. He'd been watching her every move. Had to make sure she didn't get too close.

Thank God she'd left her perch at the window and had gone to bed.

Time for him to put his plan into motion.

Tugging his cap over his head to disguise his face, he slipped from the edge of the woods, crouching low as he inched back toward her car. A little snip here, a snip there, and the brakes would be gone.

And in the morning when Grace drove to work, so would she.

Chapter Nine

Parker spent a restless night, fighting off the gut-churning feeling that Grace needed him. That she was alone at her cabin, vulnerable and in danger.

The next morning anxiety and adrenaline had him so pumped, he felt as though he could run a marathon. He wanted to speak to Grace, to make sure she was safe.

He had found her phone number in Bruno's file, and had been tempted to call her. But what would he say? That he'd be her hero? He was in the damn hospital.

During morning therapy, he shocked the physical therapist by forgoing his cane and jogging on the treadmill. She called the doctor in to watch and he, also, seemed amazed by his progress.

"That new tissue obviously worked wonders," Dr. Knightly said.

A reminder that he was alive and walking. "Yeah, too bad some of the others didn't fare so well."

The color drained from the doctor's dark skin, then irritation flashed in his eyes. "That was unfortunate."

"Has there been any explanation for the problem?" Parker asked, pushing him.

Knightly shook his head. "No, but a review board is looking into the matter. We deal with several tissue brokers and are trying to pinpoint exactly where things went wrong. Then we'll cancel our contract with them and take legal action."

That made sense. "Good."

"You still need to watch it, not overdo," Dr, Knightly said. "But I'll speak with Dr. Whitehead about releasing you to the rehab center. At this rate, you won't need to stay there long."

No, he wouldn't. His iron will would drive him to a full recovery in record time.

The doctor excused himself and Parker grabbed his cell phone and punched in the number Bradford had given him for Bruno's former partner.

"Roundtree."

"Officer Roundtree, this is Detective Parker Kilpatrick. I'd like to ask you some questions about Bruno Gardener."

"Excuse me? Didn't you just undergo surgery?"

"I'm recovering. But I'm also looking into Bruno's death."

"Why? I thought you were on medical leave."

"Bruno's sister is a nurse here in the hospital. She was attacked yesterday, and I'm helping my partner ask around, see if her inquiries into her brother's death might be motive for the attack."

"I don't know how I can help you," Roundtree said. "I've already told Captain Black everything I know."

"Were there any cases you and Bruno were working on that would have pissed someone off enough to kill Bruno?"

"Nothing that was open," Roundtree said.

"What about his parents' murder? Had

he recently discovered new clues in the case?"

A long pause. "He had a theory he was exploring, but nothing concrete."

"What was that theory?"

"Look, Kilpatrick, I don't feel at liberty to discuss this matter with you, especially over the phone."

"Then meet me. Grace's life may depend on it."

Another pause, riddled with tension, then Roundtree finally agreed. "I'll try to stop by the hospital before lunch."

He hung up and Parker checked his watch, anxious to hear what the cop had to say. Even if the information didn't lead to the person who'd attacked Grace, if it led to her parents' murderer, she would finally get closure.

His cell phone trilled and he clicked to answer. "Kilpatrick."

"Parker, it's Walsh. Listen, we just caught a break. Someone phoned in that they'd seen two teenagers dumping a corpse at a local school. We're trying to track them down now. Maybe we'll crack this case."

"How about Bruno's autopsy report?"

"Still no word."

"Forensics on the recovered bodies?"

Bradford sighed. "Two of them had tissue removed. I'm checking now to see if they were official donors."

Parker massaged his leg. "Someone could be stealing the bodies, then extracting tissue to sell."

"Maybe these gang members can tell us more." He paused. "We retrieved trace from Grace Gardener's fingertips, ran it through the system and got a hit. Juan Carlos. Bruno put him away a few months ago on a drug deal."

"Where is he now?"

"Out on parole."

"You going to pick him up?"

"We've got an APB out on him now. I'll keep you posted and be by later with those files."

Parker thanked him and hung up. Finally they were getting somewhere.

Had Juan Carlos tried to kill Grace because she was looking into her brother's death?

If so, finding the man and putting him back in jail would be the only way to keep Grace safe.

GRACE WOKE UP the next day with a plan. The fact that Bruno's autopsy was missing plagued her. Someone had intentionally made it disappear, and she intended to find out why.

Because something about his body proved that he hadn't killed himself. That had to be the answer.

She punched in Frank's number and he answered on the third ring.

"What's up this morning, Grace? Are you all right?" His voice was sluggish from fatigue and worry.

"I'm fine. But I've been thinking about Bruno's autopsy being missing. I've decided to have his body exhumed."

"Grace…" Frank wheezed a tired breath. "Are you sure you want to disturb your brother now he's been laid to rest? Maybe you should just let this thing go."

"I can't do that, Frank. I'm surprised you can."

"I'm just worried," Frank said. "I can't stand to think about someone trying to hurt you."

"I don't mean to upset you. But you were a cop, Frank. You must want the truth as much as I do."

"I do. I just don't want to lose anyone else I care about."

"I understand, and I'll be careful, Frank. I promise."

He mumbled okay, then she hung up, called the police department and asked to speak to Captain Black. Apparently, Parker or his partner had already informed him about the missing autopsy report. "I'd like to have my brother's body exhumed, Captain."

He emitted a long sigh. "Are you certain that's necessary? We all know what the original report said."

"Maybe the ME overlooked something," she argued. "And I'm curious to know if there were any changes in his body after the mix-up at the morgue."

"I'm sure the ME would have alerted us if there had been something suspicious."

"There has to be something, or why else would someone destroy the reports?"

Another long pause. "I don't know."

"Then we have to have Bruno examined again. You do want the truth about his death, don't you?"

"Of course I do." Anger and annoyance filled his tone. "But we're knee-deep in the department with all these bodies being snatched. And a woman was strangled tonight."

"I know those cases are important," Grace said, "but so was Bruno." Her voice choked and she paused to gather her composure. "Please, Captain…"

"All right. I'll start the process."

She thanked him and disconnected the call, rolling her shoulders to alleviate the tension as she headed to the shower. Her muscles were stiff and sore from her tumble down the steps the day before, but she ignored the aches as she bathed and dressed to go to the hospital.

Before she left she retrieved her photo album from the antique trunk, which had belonged to her parents, in the den. Now it doubled as a coffee table, while the quilt her mother and grandmother had hand sewn lay across the rocking chair where her father used to sit and smoke his pipe. Warm memories filled her along with the need for justice for them. She could see her mother in the old-fashioned kitchen with its checkered curtains, baking homemade apple pies and biscuits. She and Bruno would spread butter and honey on them and eat them at the beach. Then they'd carry the extras down to feed the seagulls.

For a moment she closed her eyes and could smell the tantalizing aroma of cinnamon and apples. And the pungent odor of her father's cigar….

Tears threatened to choke her, but she swallowed them back, although when she opened her eyes the room blurred. In that second, images of her father and Bruno out in the yard throwing the softball floated back. Others followed—she and her mother collecting seashells in the early morning, checking the tides for the best time to go crabbing. The time her father lost his sunglasses in the inlet and they'd joked about an alligator eating them….

She wanted her own family someday, children and pets, wanted to make those kinds of memories with them. She imagined a small towheaded little girl or a brown-haired little boy skipping down to the seashore, smiling in awe as an osprey took flight, digging in the sand to find a secret tunnel to China….

Not the kind of life she'd ever have with a cop like Parker Kilpatrick.

Why was she thinking about a family with him? She barely knew him.

Stifling the silly fantasy, she skimmed through the book, noting the photographs of her and Bruno as they'd grown up. She had checked his homework when he was little, tutored him in spelling, taught him to dance when he asked his first girlfriend to the Valentine dance, and both feared for him and encouraged him when he'd joined the police academy.

In turn, Bruno had protected her from brutes in high school because even at thirteen, he'd towered over her and had played the big brother. He had encouraged her to take out a loan to attend nursing school and they'd celebrated together after graduation.

And on the day he'd been buried, she'd promised to keep his St. Christopher medal safe and to find his killer.

She wiped her eyes, closed the photo album and placed it back in the trunk, safeguarding it with her memories and love for the family she'd lost. Then she grabbed her purse and headed to her car.

She coasted along the street from her cottage, turned onto the main road and drove toward the hospital. Parker was probably being transferred to the Coastal Island rehab facility, and she wanted to see him first.

Traffic was surprisingly light for the summer as she drove along the coast, but suddenly a Camaro pulled out in front of her. She swerved to avoid it and hit the brakes, but her car accelerated instead. She fought panic and patted them with her foot, but nothing happened.

Another car blared its horn and she

swerved back to the right side of the road, but the car skidded, she raced over the embankment and dove into the salt marsh. The impact jerked her forward and she screamed as the seat belt clenched her backward. Still, she pumped the brakes but they failed completely.

The car bounced over another rut and pitched headfirst in a pit in the marsh, jerking her forward. Her seat belt snapped, breaking, and she threw her arms in front of her to keep from hitting the steering wheel, but the impact was too strong and her body was thrown against the wheel. She braced for the air bag, but it didn't deploy, and her head slammed against the steering wheel.

Stars swam before her eyes and she tasted blood, then the world swirled into a black fog of nothingness.

HE PULLED TO THE SIDE of the embankment, parked and stared into the marsh at Grace Gardener's car, his heart racing. Just as he'd planned, the air bag hadn't deployed.

And she wasn't moving to get out.

Had she hit her head? Suffered internal injuries? Was she dead?

He rolled the cigarette between his fingers, then lit it and watched the smoke curl and float into the hazy sky as he scanned the highway. Hopefully no one would spot her crashed car from the main road, at least long enough for her to suffer.

And if she had survived, maybe she'd at least be scared enough to stop asking questions, and sticking her nose into matters that she shouldn't.

But he hoped to hell she was dead, before she discovered the truth.

He couldn't take a chance on getting caught or being exposed.

No matter who he had to kill, he'd keep his secrets….

Chapter Ten

Parker frowned as he read the morning paper. A waitress from a local café had been murdered—strangled by a pair of silk panties, and left dead in a hotel on the outskirts of town. Police had not revealed the victim's identity and reported no leads, but were investigating.

Damn. Halloween this year had brought out the worst crazies. And with this new crime, manpower would definitely be split on the force.

A knock sounded at the door and David Roundtree, Bruno's sandy-blond-haired former partner, poked his head into the room. Parker had never spent time with the undercover cop, but he recognized him from the department.

He stood and extended his hand. "Detective Parker Kilpatrick."

Roundtree introduced himself and Parker explained his concerns about Grace and her brother's death.

Roundtree sat in the stiff vinyl chair across from Parker's bed while Parker purposely remained on the edge of the bed facing him, unwilling to look like an invalid by climbing in bed. "Tell me about Bruno Gardener," Parker said.

"What do you want to know?"

"What kind of man he was. What he was working on. If he shared anything about his sister with you."

Roundtree narrowed his eyes. "What about the sister?"

"They were close?"

"Yes," Roundtree said without preamble. "He adored Grace, told me time and time again that she had helped raise him, that she was intelligent and tough, that he wished he could have spared her the pain of witnessing her parents' shooting."

"So he was still investigating their deaths?"

"Investigating? Hell, he was obsessed with solving it. Said he hated to know the killer had gone free all these years while he and Grace had been robbed of their family."

"Do you believe Bruno committed suicide?"

Roundtree sighed and crossed his ankles. "The evidence pointed to that."

Parker hardened his voice, "That's not what I asked."

Roundtree met his gaze head-on. "I didn't think he was suicidal, no. But something could have happened to trigger it that he didn't share with me."

"Grace doesn't think so."

"She's his sister. She doesn't want to believe that he would choose to leave her."

Another thought struck Parker—maybe Bruno hadn't been strong enough to handle whatever he'd discovered.

"I'm still not convinced he took his own life," Parker said. "Not if he was so obsessed with solving the case. And not if he was the protective brother I assume he was. He wouldn't have left Grace with a killer on the loose."

Roundtree chuckled sardonically. "Damn right about him being protective. He watched her like a hawk when they went out. And he was always cautioning her about strangers and the men she dated."

"Was there anyone specific that he was concerned about?"

"Not that I know of." Roundtree twisted his mouth sideways. "But he feared that the guy who killed his folks would come after Grace one day. He even thought that one day she might identify the killer."

Parker tensed. "Did Grace see the killer's face?"

Roundtree shook his head. "Not according to the reports. But who knows what really happened. She was a traumatized seven-year-old. She might have known the man."

Parker contemplated that suggestion.

Roundtree shrugged. "It was one of Bruno's theories. Although the shooting read like a professional hit."

"So someone could have hired the gunman to kill the family."

Roundtree nodded. "Exactly."

Although Juan Carlos might have killed Bruno for revenge, he hadn't spent that much time in jail for the drug charges, and had just gotten paroled. Murdering a cop was not only risky but a big jump from his prior offense.

Although the man probably needed money. What if someone hired Carlos to kill Bruno?

It could be the same man who'd killed the Gardeners.

PAIN SPLINTERED Grace's temple as she forced her eyes open, but sunshine blinded her and the world spun in a drunken haze.

Where was she? What had happened?

She brought one hand up to rub her temple and felt a sticky thick, substance. Blood. She must have hit her head.

Her breath rushed out as memories surfaced. The car swerving in front of her. Trying to avoid it. Slamming on the brakes and careening over the embankment.

The brakes not working.

The car crashing into the marsh. Her seat belt snapping. The air bag failing to deploy.

Then the darkness.

Now the car was stuck in the marsh, the nose sinking deeper into the murk.

She licked her lips and tasted blood. Panic clawed at her at the numbness in her limbs. Her legs felt heavy, her body weighty and achy. Fighting hysteria, she tried to move them and managed to wiggle her toes and one leg. Her right one was trapped beneath the warped steering wheel.

A sob wrenched her throat, but she swallowed it back, praying someone had seen her crash. But when she angled her head to look behind her, she couldn't see the road. Unless she escaped herself, no one would find her.

She inhaled. She had to save herself. Find her phone and call 9-1-1.

She glanced frantically on the seat for her purse and spotted it on the floor, the contents spilled across the mat. Determination kicked in, and she twisted and wiggled her body until she lay sideways on the seat. Her fingers touched the purse strap, but the world swirled in a haze and she closed her eyes, fighting nausea.

It took her several seconds and half a dozen deep breaths before she could open her eyes again. Sweat trickled down her neck into her shirt. Her hands shook as she grasped the purse and dragged it onto the seat.

Her compact still lay on the floor along with her brush and a package of tissues, but no phone, so she dug inside the handbag and searched for it.

Trembling, she managed to find it and flipped it open, but when she punched the connect button, nothing happened. Oh, God, the battery was dead. She must have forgotten to charge it.

Tears choked her and she threw the phone back in her bag, despair sucking at her. The car felt as if it was slipping deeper into the marsh, the heat outside radiating off the leather seats and dash.

She didn't have time to sit here and feel sorry for herself. Mentally shaking herself, she wiped at her eyes and swallowed hard. She had to make it to the road. Her legs were fine, just bruised, and even though her head was throbbing like the devil, she could walk. She would climb over the embankment to the street and flag down help.

She tried to open the door, but it was jammed, the bottom of the car sinking into the marsh. She nearly screamed in frustration. A second later she opened the window, threw her purse over her shoulder, then wiggled sideways until she managed to jerk her leg out from under the warped steering wheel. Heaving herself up onto the seat, she gripped the window frame and crawled through it.

Then she lunged forward onto the wet ground, landing on her hands and knees. Her wrist buckled and she almost collapsed, but gritted her teeth and righted herself. Her shoes sank into the water, wet sand oozing up around the soles, and she swiped the slush off her hands onto her nurse's uniform. Her breathing was choppy, and the sun blinded her, making her vision blur.

She hesitated, swayed and leaned over, bracing her hands on her knees until the world slid back into focus. Perspiration beaded on her lip and forehead, and mosquitoes buzzed and nipped at her arms and legs as she forced herself to move across the marsh. Her legs ached as the muck sucked at her feet, and her lungs begged for air, but she dragged herself onward. One step. Another. Another.

Slowly she slogged through the sea oats, the thick layers scratching her bare skin as she climbed the embankment. She was sweating and heaving for air as she finally reached the top, but she spotted the road and sheer self-preservation spurned her forward until she reached the asphalt. Her soggy shoes skidded on the gravel and shells, and she twisted her ankle, then pitched forward and collapsed at the edge of the hot pavement.

Blinking against the tears and sweat streaming down her face, she tried to scream for help, but her parched throat closed and again the world went black.

Parker paced to the window in his room, then turned to face Roundtree. "Did Bruno have any new leads on his parents' case?"

Roundtree averted his gaze, a telltale sign that he might be hiding something.

"He did, didn't he?" Parker asked.

"He didn't have anything concrete."

"Come on, spill it, Roundtree," Parker said. "What was going on?"

Roundtree glanced at the door as if to verify they were alone, then lowered his voice. "He thought that his parents were killed because his father discovered one of his fellow officers was on the take."

Parker studied his grave expression and realized Roundtree was conflicted over divulging Bruno's suspicions. Tossing around charges against co-workers for impropriety was always tricky business, but to accuse seasoned cops of something that had happened so many years ago would be near impossible to prove. And it would raise the hackles of everyone at the precinct. Getting Internal Affairs involved, having them probe into the officers' private lives and past would stir up anger, resentment and a hornet's nest of trouble.

Yet who had better access to criminals for hire than the cops who dealt with them on a daily basis, the ones who arrested them?

"Do you have a name?" Parker asked.

Roundtree shook his head. "No. The best person to ask would be Jim Gardener's old partner, Frank Johnson."

"I take it he's retired?"

Roundtree nodded. "A few years ago. But he still lives in Savannah. According to Bruno, Johnson acted as sort of a surrogate father to him and his sister."

Parker would ask Grace about the man, then he'd talk to Frank himself. And if Frank Johnson knew anything, Parker would convince him to come clean, that the only way to keep Grace safe was to finally confess the truth.

Roundtree stood to leave so Parker thanked him, then a minute later, Dr. Knightly came in, examined him and went to sign transfer papers. Parker was elated. He'd be moving back into the rehab facility, but soon he'd leave there and return to his own cabin. Back to his job full-time.

Until then he'd continue working behind the scenes.

He was packing the few meager things he'd brought with him to the hospital when Walsh poked his head in. "How're you doing?"

"Good." He told him about his release and Bradford dropped a stack of files on the bedside table.

"Here are the reports of all the bodies that went missing and were recovered. Look them over and see if you find anything that might help us catch these guys."

"I thought you were going to question those two teenagers you found unloading bodies?"

"We're still running them down. Hopefully I'll have them in custody this afternoon."

"I'd like to be there when you question those boys."

Bradford ran a hand through his hair. "Parker, I know you're anxious to get back on the streets, but you can help more by studying these files. We need a fresh eye."

Parker chewed the inside of his cheek. "All right. But did you find out if they ever enhanced that photo of the guy who attacked Grace?"

"Yes, but it was still hard to see the man's face. We showed it around the hospital but no one recognized him."

"What about Carlos?"

"We haven't found him yet."

Damn. "We need to ASAP. I have a feeling he was paid to kill Grace."

Bradford arched a brow. "Then he'll spill his guts with a little pressure."

"Exactly." He grabbed his bag and headed to the door. "I'm being released. I want to talk to Grace before I move back into the rehab center."

"I can drive you over. But I thought you had to leave here in a wheelchair."

"Over my dead body."

Walsh laughed and clapped him on the back, and they exited the room. Parker passed Dr. Knightly in the hall with his release papers, but he looked agitated, and two of the nurses hovered at the nurses' station, with frantic expressions on their faces.

"What's going on?" Parker asked.

Dr. Knightly's mouth lifted into a grimace. "It's nothing you need to concern yourself with."

"Why not? If it involves the tissue transplants—"

"It has nothing to do with that." The doctor tapped his pen on the clipboard. "It's just that Grace Gardener was brought into the ER a few minutes ago."

Parker's heart clenched. "What for?"

"She had an accident, crashed her car into the marsh."

Tension tightened every limb in Parker's body. "Is she all right?"

Seconds stretched into an eternity while Parker waited for him to answer. "She's in the ER now."

Parker didn't wait for him to elaborate. He took off as fast as his injured leg would carry him, climbed onto the elevator and held his breath until it opened at the emergency room.

He had to see Grace, had to know that she was alive.

TOO BAD Grace wasn't DOA and he could kill two birds with one stone—she'd be finished nosing into his business, and he'd take her body and cut it up and donate it to science.

Instead he slipped into the morgue and checked the toe tags. Which stiff would go next? One that hadn't already been identified or claimed? One who had no family waiting, planning their funeral?

He found the perfect specimen. An old man who had been registered as homeless. No one would care to really look for him.

And with the kids snatching bodies and painting them up for their Halloween pranks, the cops would think they had added this one to their game. A perfect cover for *him*.

He tugged his surgical mask over his face, placed the sheet over the body, gripped the gurney and pushed it through the double doors, then outside to the van he had waiting.

Chapter Eleven

Parker pushed his way into the ER, demanding to see Grace. "Where is she?"

A beefy male nurse held him back with one arm. "Sorry, sir, but you can't go in. They're working on her now."

Bradford placed a hand on Parker's back as if to contain him, but Parker shook it off. "How is she? What's her condition?"

"She's unconscious. Looks like she sustained a head injury, probably a concussion, but she should make it. They'll run tests, of course…"

Parker nodded, yet his stomach churned with anxiety. What if she'd suffered internal injuries? What if her head wound was serious and she had brain damage? Bleeding to the brain?

Worry knotted his insides, but he inhaled sharply to control his anger.

"Sounds like she'll be okay," Bradford said in a low voice.

Parker fisted his hands by his sides. "She'd better be."

"You care about her, don't you?" Bradford asked.

Parker whipped his head toward his partner. "I…" He had no idea how to answer. He did care more than he wanted to admit. But he had no future with her.

Still, he wanted to make sure she was safe. Hold her and feel her breathing and alive in his arms.

He turned back to the nurse. "Tell me what happened."

"All I know is that she had a car accident." He gestured to two paramedics exiting an exam room. "You might talk to them. They could probably tell you more."

Parker strode toward the pair and cornered the young man and woman. "You brought in Grace Gardener?"

The female, Jordan, according to her name tag, nodded. "Are you family?"

"No, a detective with the S.P.D. Can you tell me about this accident?"

"She crashed her car into the marsh," the man, Alvin, said.

"She called 9-1-1 herself?"

Jordan shook her head. "No, a woman driving by saw Miss Gardener collapsed on the side of the road. Apparently she'd dragged herself up to the highway to get help."

If she'd been walking at all, that was a good sign.

"Did she say anything on the ride over?"

The paramedic shook his head. "No, by the time we arrived, she was unconscious."

So they didn't know the details of her accident. He had to talk to Grace, find out what caused her to crash.

In light of the attempt on her life the day before, he had to wonder, though— had it really been an accident or had there been foul play?

GRACE'S HEAD FELT as if it had been sliced in two, and an irritating buzzing sound echoed in her ears. She forced her eyes open, but the lights intensified the pain splintering her temple and she closed them again, the world spinning.

Blind panic threatened to consume her. Where was she? What had happened?

She tried to speak, but her voice came out so raspy that it got lost in the hub of noise around her, so she cleared her throat and reached a shaky hand up to snag someone's sleeve. "Where am I?"

"You're in the ER, honey," a kind, low voice that she recognized as Becky Carlisle, one of her favorite nurses, said. "You had an accident. The medics brought you in."

"Accident?" She searched her memory and the horrifying last few moments before she'd crashed into the marsh returned. The car turning in front of her, the brakes failing, the realization that she might die...

"How bad?" she whispered, automatically raising her hand to her head.

"You probably have a concussion," Becky said, "and you have some bruises on your knees, arms and chest, but you should be okay. They're going to do a CAT scan, take some X-rays. You know the drill."

Grace winced, but nodded, accepting the inevitable but already anxious to be released. Though she worked in the hospital, she wasn't any more fond of being a patient than the people she treated.

Becky gently smoothed her hair away from her forehead. "There's a detective, that patient Kilpatrick, in the waiting room demanding to see you. Let me tell him you're conscious and okay."

Grace clutched Becky's arm. "Tell him to come back. I need to talk to him."

"Dr. Whitehead won't be happy about that. You know how he is. He'll want to run the tests first."

"Please, Becky, it's important."

Becky nodded, then disappeared and Grace pressed a hand over her eyes and tried to rest. A minute later Parker's gruff voice broke through the hazy blur of the ER.

"Grace?" He laid his hand over hers and squeezed her fingers, moving her hand away from her face. She opened her eyes and met his gaze. His amber eyes looked hard but worried, his expression set in granite, the scar at his temple jumping as he clenched his jaw. "Are you hurting?"

Heavens, yes, but she didn't want to alarm him. "Headache," she said softly. "It'll go away."

He made a harrumph sound. "You look like hell."

She tried to laugh but it sounded choked. "Thanks, Parker. You know how to turn a girl's head."

"I'm serious, Grace." He ran a finger over her forehead, narrowed his eyes at the gash that she knew was probably bloody and dirty.

"Good thing you didn't go into nursing," she whispered. "Your bedside manner stinks."

A small smile tugged at his mouth, then he leaned so close she felt his breath on her face. She thought he was going to say something about his bedside manner for a moment, something sexy, or maybe that was wishful thinking.

Then he murmured, "Sorry," but his tone turned brusque. "I'm not used to coddling people, especially when I'm pissed. Now tell me what happened."

She explained about the car pulling in front of her, swerving and hitting the brakes. "They wouldn't work, though," she whispered. "I kept pumping them, but nothing happened." The throbbing splitting her temple increased. "I lost control, crashed into the marsh."

"How'd you hit your head? Weren't you wearing your seat belt?"

She nodded. "Yes, I always buckle, but the belt snapped."

"What about the air bag?"

She frowned. "It didn't deploy. I…don't know why. And the brakes…I just had the car tuned up last week."

Parker's eyes flared with anger, and she realized where his train of thought was heading.

"I'll get a CSI team to examine your car with a fine-tooth comb. If there was foul play, we'll find out."

A sliver of apprehension tickled her

spine. If he was right and someone had tampered with her car, then this was the second time in two days someone had tried to kill her.

This time they'd almost succeeded.

FURY MADE PARKER grind his teeth. Grace looked so lost and vulnerable lying in that hospital bed that he wanted to crawl in with her and hold her. The medics had cut off her clothes and she wore one of the hospital gowns that he'd learned to hate, the ones that labeled a person as a patient.

Grace shouldn't be lying there hurt.

Damn. Someone had cut her brake lines—even without a crime scene unit, he'd bet his life on it.

And Grace had almost lost hers today.

He swallowed back the fear and wave of cold terror that realization brought. He didn't want to lose Grace.

Not that she was his.

But still, he couldn't let her die. She deserved to be safe, happy, to find a nice guy, get married, have babies. The kind of life a cop like him would never have, but he wanted it for her because Grace had been the angel who'd brought him back to life when he'd teetered at the edge of death's door, just as she'd done for countless others.

Grace was selfless. Kind. Loving.

He wanted to comfort her, be the friend she needed. Struggling to control his temper, he lowered his voice, stroked her hair gently from her cheek, tried to ignore the stab of fury at the blood matting the beautiful strands. "Grace, I'm sorry you were hurt. But if someone did this to you, I promise I'll find out who it is."

"Thank you, Parker. I…can't believe this is happening."

So like Grace to believe in the goodness of people when all he ever saw was the evil. "I'm sure they'll keep you overnight for observation. I'm going to talk to my partner, get a crime scene unit out to your car, but I'll be back."

She nodded, but it was obvious that fatigue and pain weighted her muscles. The nurse who'd allowed him entry appeared with Dr. Whitehead, and Parker stepped aside. "I'll see you later."

She nodded, and Whitehead approached with concern tightening his features. "We're taking you for that CAT scan now."

Knowing she was in good hands and needed medical treatment, Parker strode back through the ER, then to Walsh, where he quickly relayed Grace's story. "I want that car impounded and examined. I have a bad feeling, Walsh, that this was no accident."

Bradford nodded and immediately called the station, then explained their suspicions. When he hung up, he wore a grim expression. "The captain is sending a team to the scene now."

"Good. I hope they find some prints so we can nail this guy." He paced to the coffee machine and got a cup of coffee. Bradford followed and did the same, and they took chairs in the waiting room.

Parker took a hefty sip of the bitter brew, then spoke without preamble. "Grace needs protection."

"I'll talk to the captain," Bradford said, "but with these missing corpses, the vandalism and Halloween pranks, and now this strangling victim, the squad is stretched to the limit."

Parker extended his leg, winced, but refused to show his pain. "I can do it."

Bradford raised a brow. "Parker, you know the captain is not going to assign you as her bodyguard. You're still on disability leave."

"I'm being released today to the rehab facility. Instead, I'll go home with Grace and guard her."

Bradford shook his head, but Parker had made up his mind. "You said yourself that there's probably no one else. Better Grace have me and a gun than to be on her own. Look where that's gotten her."

Bradford gave him a skeptical look but conceded his point. "I'll talk to the captain and give you a call."

Relief surged through Parker. "Thanks, partner."

Bradford left to head to the station, but

Parker remained seated. He wasn't going anywhere, not without Grace.

From now on, he'd guard her 24/7.

THE NEXT twenty-four hours dragged by. Despite Dr. Whitehead's stern disapproval and objections, Parker spent the night in the reclining chair in Grace's room. The concussion caused her to sleep most of the time, although the nurses woke her occasionally to check her condition.

He used the idle hours to study the photos from the corpses that had been recovered after disappearing mysteriously from various morgues. He also reviewed the officers' notes.

After careful study, he noted that the same body-moving service, a small local group called Delaney's, had lost at least three of the bodies, but the service had blamed a clerical error. He made a note to ask Bradford about the body-moving service and the funeral home.

Then he studied the pictures of the bodies after they were recovered. According to the ME, there had been no significant damage or changes afterward.

Parker had seen plenty of autopsies before, so the surgical scars and stitches didn't bother him, but on two bodies he noticed similar markings along the insides of the person's thigh. On another he saw a similar slice on the man's calf and torso.

He recognized them because he had similar scars.

He phoned Bradford. "Did you find out if those victims with tissue removed were volunteer donors?"

"One was, but two were not."

Parker hissed. "So someone was stealing tissue."

"Looks that way. Now we'll have to pinpoint who."

"Perhaps there's a connection between the body snatchers and the body-moving service or funeral home."

"I'm on it," Bradford agreed.

"What happened with those teens you were going to question?" Parker asked.

Bradford sighed. "They admitted to stealing three bodies, the Douglas woman,

Cantrell man and Sorenson lady, but said it was a Halloween prank. Apparently they belong to a gang who call themselves the Skulls. There's a rival group named the Crossbones who started the competition."

"How did they get access to the bodies?" Parker asked.

"One of their buddies, a guy who likes to call himself Frankenstein, ripped off some surgical scrubs. Said he just slipped in at night and took the bodies from the crypt at the hospital."

"Damn. They need better security."

"Where are the kids now?"

"They're in custody, but the parents have lawyers so I expect I'll have to cut them loose soon."

"Did you ask if they stole Bruno's body?"

"Yeah, but neither one of the two I have in custody owned up to it. I'm trying to locate the leader of the Crossbones so I can bring him in for questioning."

"Good. Let me know when you do."

Bradford blew out a breath. "I also had our team compare Juan Carlos's mug shot with the picture from the security tape. It's hard to tell, but we think it may be him."

"Any word on his whereabouts?"

"No, we're still looking."

Parker sighed and pulled his hand down his chin. "We have to find him and make him tell us who hired him."

"I know. But he's an expert at hiding. It took the cops months to nail him before."

Parker didn't want this to drag on for months. Not with Grace's life hanging in the balance.

"How's the Gardener woman?" Bradford asked.

Parker glanced at her sleeping form. She'd woken twice with nightmares and he'd comforted her. He wanted to cradle her in his arms, make sure she never suffered again.

"Resting. What did you learn about her car?"

Bradford made a sound of disgust. "You were right. The brake lines were cut. The air bag had been tampered with and the seat belt nearly severed. That's why it snapped when she crashed and the reason for the head injury."

Hearing his fears confirmed made Parker's gut clench with fury. If Juan Carlos had done this, Parker would kill him.

He'd also find out who had hired the bastard, then he'd track that son of a bitch down and take care of him, as well.

HE HAD TO get out of town.

He stuffed his extra shirt and jeans into his duffel bag, grabbed his shaving kit and packed it, then scrubbed a hand over his newly shaven jaw. He missed the thick mane he'd grown in the pen, but he had to alter his appearance in case anyone had seen him around Grace Gardener's car.

He was a pro, though; the cops wouldn't find any prints.

No, he wasn't stupid. He'd made mistakes in his drug-running days, trusted the wrong people, left evidence, but eighteen months in the joint had taught him a lot about who to team up with and who not to.

Cursing the sweat rolling down his neck and back, he punched in his contact number. "I need my final payment."

"You took care of Miss Gardener?"

"I did what you asked." Although he'd meant to kill her. But damn, the woman was persistent and wouldn't die.

He would take care of her, though; he had to. He couldn't leave any loose ends behind.

"The money is exactly where I said it would be."

He fingered the key to the locker at the boathouse. "If it's not, you know I'll be back. And you won't fare as well as the woman."

"It's there," the man said harshly. "And remember, if you get caught, you're on your own."

"I'm not going to get caught," he said. "But if you do, the same thing goes. Talk, and you're a dead man."

Chapter Twelve

Grace's eyes felt gritty, and her body ached all over. She had no idea how long she'd slept. It seemed like an eternity, and she was disoriented as to the time of day, but one thing gave her solace—every time she'd awakened, she'd seen Parker sitting in the chair beside her bed. Knowing that he guarded over her allowed her to put her nightmares at bay long enough to give her body the reprieve it desperately needed after the accident.

Finding peace of mind was a different story. Even in sleep, she'd been conscious that her life was in danger. That somehow by the grace of God, she'd been spared the day before, but that her number might be up any moment.

She didn't want to die. Not alone. Not without knowing a man's love or a baby's tug at her breast. She wanted marriage, love, children and a happily-ever-after that had been stolen from her parents and her when she was seven.

And from her brother just a few short months ago.

By noon, she sat up, unable to sleep any more and antsy to leave the hospital.

Parker closed the folder he'd been reading and gave her a concerned look. "How are you feeling?"

"Better," she said honestly. "I hope they'll let me go home soon."

"What? Don't tell me you hate hospitals?"

She laughed at his dry humor. "Just when I'm a patient."

A small grin tugged at his mouth. "I know what you mean. I'm ready to get out of here myself."

She adjusted the hospital gown and tugged the blanket over her lap. "Did they release you?"

He nodded. "I can check into the rehab facility anytime."

"Then what's keeping you?"

"You." His gaze met hers, emotions simmering beneath the steamy surface of his eyes. That and an undercurrent of sexual tension.

Or maybe she was imagining the predatory look because of her own fantasies.

"Parker, I appreciate you staying here with me, but I'm all right now."

He made a grunting noise. "Yeah, until the next time this maniac comes after you."

She bit down on her lip and twisted the covers between her fingers. A second later Parker moved to the bed and sat beside her, then lifted her chin with his thumb, forcing her to look at him.

"I'm not going to let him get you, Grace. I promise."

The sound of someone clearing his throat intruded on the moment and Parker pivoted to find Dr. Whitehead watching. "Mr. Kilpatrick?"

Parker stood and walked to the

window, putting distance between him and Grace. "Doctor."

Grace bit back a smile at his clipped tone. If Wilson hadn't interrupted, what would have happened?

Would Parker have kissed her?

PARKER CLENCHED his hands by his sides in frustration, silently chastising himself for nearly kissing Grace. If Whitehead hadn't walked in when he had, Parker would have pulled her into his arms and tasted her.

Damn it, he *wanted* to taste her bad.

But he had to restrain himself. Grace might be vulnerable, needy, frightened, but he had no right to take advantage of that vulnerability.

Especially when he had nothing to offer her but protection as a cop.

The sight of the suave, rich, Dr. White-head was enough to ground him in reality. Although Parker didn't like the possessive way the man was looking at Grace, as if he could eat her up like cotton candy.

Hell, whether the captain approved or

not, he was going to protect Grace. He had
nothing *but* time on his hands, and he
would use it to keep Grace safe.

Grace threw off the covers and swung
her legs over the side of the bed. It was the
first time he'd seen her legs bare, and he
couldn't help but admire their slender,
muscular shape.

"Dr. Whitehead," Grace said. "I hope
you intend to release me now."

"Are you sure you're ready to go
home, Grace? You suffered quite a blow
to the head."

"Yes, Wilson. I'll rest better in my own
bed than in the hospital, and we both know
it."

"But the hospital has security," Whitehead said. "And there are people to take
care of you if you need something."

Parker grimaced. And Whitehead was
here. He didn't say it, but obviously he
would be looking in on Grace, personally
seeing to her care.

"She won't be alone," Parker cut in.
"Grace needs a bodyguard and I'm
taking the job."

Grace gaped at him, stunned into silence while Whitehead glared at him as if he were an alien. An incompetent one at that.

"You're hardly in a position to take care of anyone," Whitehead said harshly.

"I'm well enough to be released," Parker argued. "Besides, from what I've seen so far, your hospital security is lacking. Grace was first attacked here, you know."

Whitehead's look turned lethal but he couldn't argue the point.

"Parker, I appreciate the offer," Grace murmured, "but it's not necessary—"

"The subject is not up for debate," Parker said brusquely. "My partner confirmed that your brake lines were cut, Grace. Someone caused you to crash yesterday. It was no accident. And so far we haven't identified or found the man who attacked you in the stairwell. We haven't even found a company that uses the logo from the man's uniform in the picture, so it had to be bogus."

Grace paled, stirring guilt in Parker's

chest. But Grace needed to know the truth so she would be alert. So she would accept his help.

And so they could catch the bastard who'd put her in the hospital and nearly put her in the ground like her brother.

GRACE ALWAYS kept a change of clothes in her locker at the hospital, so she changed into the cotton skirt, tank top and sandals before being dismissed. Then she and Parker caught a cab to his cabin at CIRP's rehab facility for him to pack a bag and retrieve his gun. He felt naked without it, he'd said. While she waited in the taxi, she called her insurance company to arrange for a rental car. At the rental car place, she chose a Corolla, but Parker insisted on driving, reminding her that she'd suffered a concussion only twenty-four hours earlier.

It felt odd to relinquish control to him, yet almost natural, more natural than she wanted to admit. She could get used to having someone to lean on, alleviate the burden she'd carried all her life.

Yet Parker was a cop, not the kind of man to settle down with a family, not the kind to stick around.

"Do you need to stop anywhere before we go to your cottage?" he asked.

"Maybe the grocery store. I…don't know what you like to eat."

He reached across the console and laid his hand over hers. "I don't expect you to cook for me or wait on me, Grace. I'm not an invalid. I'm here to take care of you."

Maybe they could take care of each other. The offer teetered on the edge of her tongue, but she bit it back. "I don't know what to say, Parker. You really don't have to do this."

"Yes, I do," he said in a gruff voice. "At least until whoever tried to kill you is in prison where he belongs."

She sighed and tried to ignore the tingling in her hand where he was touching her, tried to stifle the desire building inside her, the need to have more with this man. To ask him to stay because he wanted to be with her, wanted to hold her, kiss her, join her in bed.

But he'd made his intentions clear, and she had to accept them. She knew better than anyone the instincts ingrained in cops, that she couldn't change the man beneath the badge.

She admired that man, but she couldn't live with what he did—not after losing her family because of it.

She needed someone safe. Someone who would be around every day, who would come home in the evenings and share dinner with her, who wouldn't keep her up at night worrying if he was dead or alive.

Someone like Wilson.

So why hadn't she accepted any of his overtures? Why didn't she tingle and feel the stirrings of desire, the heat, when he touched her hand?

Parker stopped at a grocery store and they gathered a few essentials, along with some pasta, fresh fish and a bottle of wine. When they were back in the car, Parker spoke again. "I know you said you live on Tybee, but you'll have to give me directions to your cottage."

She pointed out the streets as he drove onto the island.

"How did you end up on Tybee?" he asked.

She breathed in the scent of the ocean, the palm trees, heard the gentle cicadas in the distance, the water rushing to the shore. Its familiarity resurrected sweet memories. "My parents owned this cottage," she said. "They used to bring me and Bruno here when we were small."

"So this was a second home?"

She nodded. "My father was a cop, too, you know. He and mom needed a place to get away from it all."

"How did your father afford two houses on a cop's salary?"

Anger knotted her insides. "What are you suggesting, Parker? That my father was a dirty cop?"

"Not at all, just curious."

She flexed her fingers, realizing she'd sounded defensive. "The cottage belonged to my grandparents. When they died, they willed it to my dad. It had been his childhood home so he couldn't bear to sell it."

"It means a lot to you, too."

His observation surprised her. "Yes. It holds a lot of happy family memories for me. The four of us used to take long walks on the beach together, build sandcastles, collect shells. My mother strung them together to make me a necklace when I was three." Her voice broke as her mother's smiling face flashed in her mind.

"I thought your parents were killed at home?" he asked quietly.

"They were, but at our other house in Atlanta, not here." Their bloody images replaced the fond ones so quickly that it choked her breath. "I guess that makes this cabin even more special. It's the only place I remember truly being happy." The admission brought tears to her eyes, but she blinked them away. "Sorry. I guess you didn't need to hear all that."

He veered into her drive, pulled to a stop and then turned to face her. "I'm glad you told me. You should be happy, Grace. And you will be again one day when this is over...."

The inside of the car suddenly closed

around her, seemed to cocoon them into their own world. The scent of his shampoo and body filled the space, drawing her into a seductive spell.

She licked her lips, wanted him to kiss her, ached to pull him closer and feel his body next to hers.

As if he felt the same intense draw, he reached for her, slid his hand up around her neck, threaded his fingers in her hair and dragged her toward him. The air simmered with hunger, with the raw need building between them.

She whispered his name, her voice vibrating with the husky plea for him to mold his mouth to hers, and he complied. With a whispered sigh of acquiesce, he lowered his head and claimed her mouth with his.

He tasted like need and man and the headiest combination of sin that made her mouth water for more, so she slid her arms around his neck and told him so with a low moan of pleasure.

PARKER PLUNGED his tongue into Grace's mouth, emboldened by the low throaty sounds she emitted, sounds that reverberated with need and hunger.

A hunger he felt all the way to his soul.

He had never wanted a woman the way he wanted Grace, had never ached to hold her and kiss her, to feel her in his arms, to give her pleasure and hear her cry his name.

But he wanted more, of course. He wanted all of Grace. Grace in his arms, Grace in his bed, Grace in his life….

Tensing, he ordered himself to pull away. He couldn't allow her to breach the barrier he'd erected so long ago, the one that made it possible for him to maintain enough objectivity to do his job.

His job was the only thing that mattered.

Until Grace…

His resistance shattered, he deepened the kiss, savoring the way her soft body brushed his, the way her breasts touched his chest, the way her tongue danced with his. Her hair glided through his fingers like fine silk as he pulled her closer, and the scent of her body made him insane with desire.

He had to get her inside the cottage. Take off her clothes. Feel her bare skin against his fingertips. Taste the delicate skin of her neck…and lower.

A horn blared, startling them both and they jerked apart, both pivoting at the same time as if they'd been caught naked in the middle of a public park. A black pickup sat behind them, a hefty gray-haired man with a frown on his face glaring at Parker.

"Oh, goodness…" Grace dropped her head forward with a sigh.

"Who in the hell is that?" Parker asked.

"Frank Johnson. He's a family friend, used to work with my dad." She released her grip from where she'd been clutching his shirt as if she wanted to tear it off.

He wanted her to tear it off. Wanted this man to disappear so they could finish what they'd begun.

But Frank climbed out and stalked toward him. The man was ticked off.

Damn. The kiss he'd shared with Grace was probably the last one he would get tonight.

Resigned, Parker opened the car door

and headed around the front of the car to help Grace, but Frank beat him to it.

"Grace, good God, are you okay? I called the hospital to talk to you and found out you'd been admitted." He gripped her arms and looked her up and down as if to check for injuries. "Why didn't you call me?"

"I'm fine, Frank." Grace spoke softly, but the smile in her voice told Parker that she had affection for the man. "I did have an accident, and a minor concussion, but as you can see, I'm okay."

"What I see are bruises on your forehead and pale skin." He hugged her to him. "Don't you know how crazy with worry I've been? I couldn't stand it if I lost you."

"I'm sorry, Frank, I didn't want to upset you. That's why I didn't call."

Frank's skin turned ruddy as he finally released Grace and glared at Parker. "Who is this?" he asked Grace.

Grace introduced him, and Parker extended his hand. "Nice to meet you, sir. I'm a detective with the S.P.D. I've heard about your years of service."

Frank stiffened but accepted the hand-shake. "Really?"

"Yes, sir."

"What are you doing here with Grace?"

Suspicion laced Frank's voice, making Parker wonder if his instant dislike of Parker was because he was kissing Grace or because he was a cop.

Grace gave Parker a pleading look as if to ask him not to tell Frank the truth, but Parker didn't believe in mincing words. Besides, Bruno's partner Roundtree had told him to talk to Frank about the Gardeners' murder. "I'm playing bodyguard to Grace." He quickly explained that her accident was no accident, but another attempt on her life.

Frank scrubbed a hand over the thick tufts of his hair, spiking the ends in scattered directions. "I told you to stop poking around, Grace. Now I hope you'll listen."

Parker squared his shoulders. "That's not going to happen. I'm on the case now, and I intend to find out who tried to kill Grace. If it has to do with Bruno's death or her parents', then I'll find those answers, as well."

Frank shifted onto the balls of his feet, turning to Grace as if to dismiss Parker. "Grace, if you need protection, I'll call one of my buddies. You don't need this man here. He'll only bring more danger to your door."

"Mr. Johnson—"

Grace threw up a hand to stop Parker from arguing. She must have sensed the tension between the two men and meant to diffuse it, but Parker refused to allow anyone to intimidate him.

Roundtree had admitted that Bruno suspected his father had discovered a cop on his squad was on the take.

Could that cop have been Frank, Mr. Gardener's own partner?

Chapter Thirteen

Grace had to dispel the tension between Parker and Frank. Ever since her parents had died, and then Bruno, Frank had been protective of her, so she'd have expected him to welcome a cop as her bodyguard.

But he obviously disapproved of Parker.

She massaged her temple where her earlier headache pulsed again. Between her injury and the sun pounding down on her, she was beginning to feel lightheaded. "Guys, can we please take this inside? The heat is getting to me."

Parker placed a hand behind her back to guide her inside. "Sorry. You should be resting."

Frank's lips thinned. "Of course, Grace."

She led the way and unlocked the door,

dropping her purse on the end table as she entered. Parker helped her settle on the couch, then hurried back to the car to retrieve the groceries while Frank claimed a seat beside her.

He folded her hands between his. "Can I get you anything, Grace?"

"No, I really am okay. You should be with Kelly, not worrying about me."

"Miss Evie is sitting with her now. I told her I wouldn't be long, but I had to talk to you."

Parker busied himself by storing her groceries in the adjoining kitchen, and Frank leaned closer to her and lowered his voice. "He seems to be moving in on you. Are you sure you can trust him, Grace?"

She wasn't sure whether to laugh at his possessive fatherly tone or to be angered by his lack of trust in her judgment. "Yes, Frank. In case you didn't read about him in the paper, he's a local hero. He's spent the last few months undergoing surgery and then rehab because he raced into a fire to save a woman's life."

Frank's expression remained grave.

"Admirable, I suppose. But if he was just released from the hospital, he may not be well enough to protect you."

"He's one of the strongest men I've ever met," Grace said earnestly.

Parker stepped into the room and cleared his throat. "Groceries are put away."

It was such a domestic thing to say that she suddenly felt an intimate connection with him. That and knowing that he'd be sleeping in her home brought an uncharacteristic blush to her face.

Although when Parker faced Frank, tension radiated between them, sparking a seed of dread to sprout in her belly.

"I've been wanting to talk to you, Mr. Johnson," Parker said.

"It's Frank."

Parker nodded. "All right, Frank."

"What's this about?" Frank asked.

"Do you know a guy named Juan Carlos?"

Frank scrunched his nose in thought. "No. Should I?"

"He's spent time in jail for drugs. Bruno put him there."

"So you think he shot Bruno out of revenge?"

Parker shrugged. "Either that or someone paid him to kill Bruno."

Frank studied him silently, his gray brows bunching together. "Any idea who would hire him?"

"I've spoken with Bruno's partner, David Roundtree. He thinks that Bruno found a lead involving his parents' murder case."

Frank wiped at a drop of sweat trickling down the side of his neck. "What kind of lead?"

Grace's heart raced. Had Bruno actually discovered the identity of her parents' killer?

PARKER WAS WALKING a fine line. Accusing, even insulting, Frank Johnson, a noted retired cop who had been well thought of in Savannah, was a dicey move. Frank had the power to turn the brass against Parker.

And accusing Frank of impropriety, of even suggesting he might have been involved in Grace's parents' murder, meant hurting Grace.

But he had never backed down from an investigation, no matter how sticky. And he couldn't now. He wanted the truth, and Grace deserved answers.

If it took pissing off Frank to solve the mystery, he would do it.

"Parker, what did Bruno find out?" Grace asked.

Eagerness laced her voice, and he prayed he didn't destroy her faith in him. "Bruno suspected that your parents were killed because your father discovered an officer on the force was on the take."

Grace gasped, but Parker studied Frank's stoic expression. His eyes didn't reflect an ounce of surprise or anger.

"Of course the police looked at that possibility years ago," Frank said in a level voice. "But Internal Affairs conducted a thorough investigation and discovered no improper conduct."

"That doesn't mean that it didn't exist,"

Parker said. "You and I both know the drill. Cops cover for their own."

"Not against a rat," Frank said. "Back then, our guys had morals, not like you youngsters today."

Parker chuckled. "We're all cut from the same cloth. I'd be interested in seeing the reports from IA."

Frank shrugged. "Suit yourself. But it's a waste of time. I could vouch for every guy who worked in that unit."

Parker narrowed his eyes. "And I suppose they'd do the same for you?"

Anger flared in the older man's eyes. "Just what are you implying, Kilpatrick?"

"You were the closest person to your partner. Yet you seemed to have no idea who might have killed the couple."

"I gave the officers in charge the names of every perp Jim had arrested."

"And you worked the case?"

Frank stood, his jowls puffing out with indignation. "Of course I did. Jim was not only my partner, but my best friend. I wanted to find his killer more than anyone else."

"Yet you could have also covered up evidence if you'd wanted." Parker lowered his voice to a lethal tone. "And I heard that you have a handicapped daughter. Your medical bills must be sky-high."

Frank balled his hand into a fist and lunged at Parker. "How dare you accuse me of impropriety!"

"Frank, please don't." Grace grabbed his arm before he could punch Parker.

Frank's breath wheezed out as he struggled for control. "Yes, I have a handicapped daughter whose health is failing," Frank snapped. "I love her dearly, and I worked two jobs to support her. But the Gardeners were—are—family to me. I practically helped raise Bruno and Grace myself after their parents died."

Maybe he did think of them as family. Or maybe he'd helped raise them because he was responsible for their parents' death?

GRACE STUDIED Parker, her emotions pingponging back and forth between anger and disbelief. Frank had left in a whir of fury.

Surely, Parker didn't really think that Frank, the man who'd been best friends with her father, the man she'd become to think of as family—the only family she had left—was capable of having her parents' killed in cold blood. Or that Frank might have had Bruno murdered.

No…she couldn't believe Frank was capable of hurting either her or her brother.

Not the man who'd ridden her piggyback across the beach when the sand had burned her feet from the afternoon heat. Not the man who'd taken pictures at her high school graduation and cheered for Bruno at his baseball games.

Not the man she'd grown to love and depend on for moral support over the years.

Needing time to settle her nerves, she walked outside onto the back patio, lifting her hair off of her neck to feel the breeze drifting from the ocean beyond the scattered trees. The sun faded into the distant horizon, streaking the sky with orange and red lines. The path through the sea oats would guide her down to the beach for a walk, and she ached to follow it, to jog along the shoreline, to release the tension tightening every cell in her body.

"Grace?"

She stiffened, Parker's accusations toward Frank echoing in her head.

"Are you all right?"

She forced a nod, although she didn't quite know how to answer that question. She'd lost so much to violence—her family, her brother, her innocence. And now the violence had directly touched her, threatened to destroy any future she might have.

He slid his hands over her arms and stroked her bare skin. "I'm sorry if I upset you by questioning Frank."

Feeling claustrophobic, panicked and torn between screaming at Parker that he'd been wrong about Frank, or throwing herself into his arms, she stepped off the patio onto the path leading to the beach.

"Grace—"

"I need some air."

"I'm going with you."

She froze, then turned to face him. "I need to be alone."

"Sorry, Grace." His gaze met hers. "That's not going to happen. Not until I catch whoever tried to kill you."

The conviction in his tone warned her not to bother arguing. So she relented and gestured for him to come with her. The night sounds of the seagulls and the water lapping against the shore calmed her as they walked along the edge of the water. Breathing in the salt air and feeling the gentle whisper of the wind against her arms and legs soothed her nerves, obliterating memories of the crash.

"I see why you like it here," Parker said. "It's peaceful, quiet."

"When I was a kid, we'd chase the waves," Grace said, smiling as sand squished into her sandals and tickled her feet. "Once Bruno and I sculpted a sand shark that was so big the local reporters photographed it. Frank helped us build it," she finished, her voice breaking.

"I had to question him," Parker said matter-of-factly. "I'm sorry it upset you, but I had to ask."

"I can't believe that he'd ever hurt me or Bruno." She hugged her arms around herself as she faced him.

His dark gaze skated over her, his eyes intense and probing, then he tucked a strand of her windswept hair behind her ear. "You trust him," Parker said simply.

She nodded, her pulse racing at his touch. "He's been there for me for years."

"Then I hope he is innocent," Parker said quietly. "But if he's not, Grace, I'll find that out."

She swallowed back an argument, knowing that he was just doing his job. He'd vowed to help her find the truth, and Parker was the type of man to keep his word.

Unable to help herself, the memory of that kiss in the car returned to taunt her. He had been hot and seductive, and she hadn't wanted him to stop.

His eyes heated now as if he were re-membering the moment, as well.

The air suddenly vibrated with sexual tension, also bringing her his scent, a musky smell that made her stomach clench with desire. Raw masculinity emanated from him as he stepped closer to her, lifted a thumb and traced it along her cheek. The moon slowly emerged in the sky and painted his strong jaw in a soft glow, but the look in his eyes seemed wolfish and primal.

She took a step toward him, so close now that her breasts brushed his chest, so close that she felt the quiver of his body and his hard sex press into her thigh. He groaned, then dragged her into his arms.

She fell into him and fused her mouth with his.

PARKER MELDED his mouth with Grace's, need driving him to pull her closer and slide his hand down her back to cup her waist. His sex hardened, aching for her touch, as she leaned into him, and he deepened the kiss, flicking his tongue along her lips and teeth, then dipping between her parted lips. She tasted like the most delicate wine, rich with flavor, exotic and so damn sweet that he craved more.

Forgetting reason and that he was supposed to be doing a job, he stroked her back, moving against her so he fit himself between her thighs. Her feminine fragrance intoxicated him, fueling his hunger. He dragged his mouth from hers, then lowered his head and dropped kisses along her jaw, then her neck, sucking gently on her skin. She moaned and threaded her fingers in his hair, her breath escaping in soft pants.

The ocean roaring behind them mimicked his heartbeat as he traced fingers over her breast, cupping her in his hand. Emboldened by her soft moan, he flicked her nipple with his thumb. She whimpered his name, and he reached beneath her tank top, slid her bra aside and stroked her nipple to a hard peak.

He wanted her clothes off. Wanted to feel every inch of her bare skin against his. Wanted to make love to her until she cried out in pleasure and forgot the pain of her past.

But a twig snapped somewhere in the distance and rational thought threatened to intercede. He started to pull away, but she clutched his shoulders and held him to her, offering him a tantalizing treat by flicking her tongue along his neck and ear.

"Grace…"

She dug her nails into his back. "Shh, don't stop."

Her encouraging words tore a hole in his resistance and he swept his mouth down to her breast, flicked his tongue over the turgid peak, then drew it into his mouth and sucked the tip.

Hunger surged through him, raw and primal. He had to have her now.

He gripped the lower edge of her tank to lift it over her neck, but suddenly a popping noise echoed in the wind.

A second later he realized the sound was gunfire, then a bullet zoomed past his head and landed in the sand at his feet.

Chapter Fourteen

"What's happening?" Grace shouted.

"Someone's shooting at us!" He pulled her into the crook of his arm, then grabbed her hand, and they ran back up the path toward the cottage. Another gunshot hit the sand below his feet and Grace screamed, stumbling.

He caught her, half dragging her up the hill and trying to shield her with his body at the same time he searched for the shooter.

Another bullet hit the tree next to his head and he pushed Grace behind it, then pivoted toward the direction of the gunshots. Narrowing his eyes, he quickly skimmed the beach, the dock to the right, deciding the shooter might be hiding behind the post of the wooden bridge leading from the neighboring house to the beach.

He spotted movement, pulled out his gun and took aim, but then the image disappeared.

"Run to the house," he ordered Grace. "I'm going after this guy."

Grace clutched his arm in a death grip. "No, Parker, you might get hurt."

Parker cupped her face between his hands. "Don't worry about me, Grace, I'll be fine. Now go."

"Parker—"

"Run," Parker ordered. "Lock the door and don't let anyone in until I get there."

Worry flickered in her eyes, but she nodded then turned and hurried toward the cottage. He slipped into the palm trees bordering Grace's property, weaving in a zigzag pattern in case the shooter was watching him, inching his way toward the neighboring yard. Grace's house sat at the end of the street in a cove, the other neighbor's house a quarter of a mile away.

The wooden bungalow looked deserted

and weathered, as if it had seen too many storms and barely survived, the yard was unkempt, and there were no cars in sight. He hunkered down, maneuvering through the sea oats, padding softly so as not to alert the shooter of his approach. Thankfully, the wind drowned out the sound of the shells crunching beneath his feet. His leg throbbed but he ignored the pain and made his way down to the dock, creeping between the vegetation.

But when he reached the dock, the shooter was gone.

Panic squeezed the air from his lungs. What if he'd followed Grace up to the house and had her now?

GRACE RACED back up the path, her heart pounding with fear. What if the shooter killed Parker?

She didn't want him to die.

She wanted another kiss, to have him hold her all night and make her forget that someone was trying to end her life.

Her lungs begged for air as she reached the patio, but a sound jarred her and she spun around to check the side of the house. A soda can rolled across the clamshelled drive, clattering noisily as it slammed into the brick edging of the flower garden.

Had the wind tossed it on the ground or had someone bumped it when they'd run by? And where had it come from? It wasn't the type of soda she drank.

Fear knotted her insides. She didn't know whether to go inside the house or to hide outside. Maybe she should go to the car. But there she'd be a sitting duck.

Parker's orders echoed in her head—go inside and lock the door.

Surely the shooter couldn't have beaten her up to the house. Not from the neighboring yard.

Trembling with each labored breath she took, she glanced around for something to use for protection, saw a small stick by the edge of the patio, snatched it and wielded it like a weapon. Easing open the door, she paused to listen for an intruder, poised to run to the car or woods should she hear a sound.

But her house sounded eerily silent, and a chill crept up her spine as if a ghost had just passed by. The whistle of the ocean breeze shattered the silence as she tiptoed inside. Senses honed, she locked the door, then quickly scanned the living room/kitchen combination. Empty.

Gripping the stick tightly in her hand, she inched toward the bedroom, well aware of every squeak and groan the wood floors made beneath her sandals. She flipped on the light switch by the door, throwing light into the room.

No one was inside. Thank God.

Suddenly a loud pounding caused her breath to catch. She froze, swallowing hard as she reached for the phone. Holding it in one hand to call 9-1-1 and the stick in the other, she slowly crept back to the den. The pounding shook the sliding-glass doors.

"Grace! Grace, it's Parker. Let me in."

Relief surged through her and she dashed toward the sliding glass doors, then threw the lock. Parker vaulted inside and dragged her into his arms.

PARKER'S BREATH whooshed out in relief. "Are you all right, Grace?"

She nodded against his chest. "I was so scared he'd shot you."

He inhaled her fragrance and stroked her back, hating that she was trembling. "I'm fine. You didn't see him near the house?"

"No. Did you get a look at him?"

"No, he was gone by the time I reached the dock." He wanted to keep holding her, but his cop instincts kicked in, along with self-recriminations. For God's sake, he'd been practically undressing her on the beach.

And the shooter had been watching.

Damn it. He should have been doing his job. Instead he'd lost his objectivity, let down his guard and nearly gotten Grace killed.

He couldn't live with her death on his conscience.

Slowly he extracted himself from her. "I'm going to call my partner. I want the beach searched for those bullets. They might lead us to the shooter."

Grace nodded and wrapped her arms

around her waist as Parker punched in Walsh's number and explained about the attack.

"I'll get some guys out there ASAP," Bradford said. "By the way, Bruno's body is being exhumed in the morning. It'll be interesting to see what we find."

Parker glanced at Grace, knowing that exhumation must be difficult on her.

"I also heard from the hospital," Bradford said. "They've traced the problematic tissue to a tissue bank called L-Tech. I'm going to question that body-moving service. The ME looked at the photos of those victims you red-flagged and they did have tissue removed. Apparently his assistant handled those cases and either didn't catch it or let it slide. We're going to talk to him, too."

"Call me. I'd like to be there when you interrogate them."

Silence stretched over the line. "Look, man, the Captain's barely approved you playing bodyguard, but you have to take it easy. Don't you have your hands full guarding Grace?"

His hands were full with her, had been all over her when they'd been shot at. A mistake he couldn't repeat.

Still, as he watched her in the kitchen preparing dinner, emotions crowded his chest. The scene was so domestic it made him yearn for it to be real. He'd never seen his own mother bake cookies or a home-made meal. In fact, she'd run out and left him and his dad when he was a toddler, so he couldn't remember her at all.

Memories of wanting, needing someone to comfort him, to love him after his injuries, raced back.

A futile thought. He didn't know how to be in a relationship. Once his mother had skipped, his father had been angry all the time. Had turned out to be as mean as a snake, using his fists instead of words to talk. Feeding himself on a liquid diet of booze every night. Parker had learned to stay out of the way, seen but not heard.

Until he'd hit his teenage years. Then he'd rebelled and become as mean as his old man. But he'd looked into the mirror one day and seen his father's reflection, and known he was becoming just as big a bastard.

He'd had to change. Putting away the very kind of man his father was had become his life.

Now he was nothing without his job. And Grace *was* the job.

Getting personally involved with her meant a distraction. Putting her life in jeopardy.

Something he couldn't do.

"Any word on that local gang Crossbones?" he said, changing the subject.

"Not yet."

"How about the waitress who was murdered?"

"Nothing concrete. Raul Cortez caught the case. He's interviewing family members and her friends now. Uniforms have canvassed the area surrounding the café where she works and the area where her body was discovered. Now, I'll get those guys out there to search for the bullets."

Parker thanked him, then hung up. If the bullets had come from the same gun that had killed Bruno, then they could prove that Grace's brother hadn't committed suicide, as Grace suspected, but that he had been murdered.

THE AIR VIBRATED with tension as Grace sliced vegetables for a salad. Not that she was hungry at all, but she needed something to do while Parker conferred with his partner. Ten minutes later two officers arrived, and she and Parker took them down to the beach to show them where to search for the bullet casings from the shooter.

Parker kept her close to his side, his gaze guarded, constantly checking the dunes and trees in case the shooter still lurked nearby.

"He may have been hiding behind the dock over there." Parker pointed to the neighboring property. "Look for footprints, trace evidence, anything you can find. The house appears to be deserted, but someone could have broken in and been staying there."

The officers nodded, then one began

combing the beach while the other traced his way over to the neighboring dock. Parker clutched his hand around her arm and coaxed her back up the path and inside the house. As they entered, he ordered her to stay in the kitchen while he swept the cottage again to make certain the shooter hadn't slipped into the house while they'd walked down to the beach.

Nerves tightened her stomach. She still couldn't believe that someone wanted her dead.

Parker's boots pounded the floor as he strode back to her. His expression looked grim, his jaw set so tightly, she could see a vein in his neck throb. And the scar on his forehead had reddened with anger.

"Parker—" She reached for him, wanted him to hold her again, but he threw up a hand, warding her off.

"What happened earlier was a mistake," he said through gritted teeth. He met her gaze head-on with a hard, cold look in his eyes. "It can't happen again, Grace."

Hurt splintered through her. She didn't understand. She thought he'd wanted her just as much as she'd wanted him. Had she misread the signs?

Any man might take an offer if a woman threw herself at him.

No, she didn't believe that. He was the most noble, honorable man she'd ever met. Although he had been hospitalized for a long time, had been without female company… "Parker—"

"I mean it, Grace. I'm here as a bodyguard and nothing else."

"That's not what it felt like earlier," she snapped.

"Yeah, and look what happened. I almost got you killed."

Emotions thickened his voice, making her wonder if he did care. But she refused to beg a man to love her.

Arguing with him seemed futile. He'd made his decision, and one thing she'd learned about Parker over the past few months of his therapy, that when he made up his mind about something, no one in hell could change it.

"Fine," she said sharply. "I'll try not to throw myself at you again."

PARKER KNOTTED his hands into fists to keep from reaching for Grace as she strode into the kitchen. He hated to hurt her, but he had to stay focused. Losing his objectivity meant endangering her, and that wasn't a chance he could take again.

No matter how difficult it was to keep his hands off of her.

While she finished preparing dinner, he accessed the files on her parents' case, then searched for information on the IA investigation. But as Frank had said, nothing incriminating had turned up—or at least nothing that was noted in the files.

He spent the next hour researching the cops who'd worked with Frank and Grace's father. One of the guys, Roger Buckingham, had died of a heart attack three years earlier, and Earl McKendrick was in a nursing home suffering from Huntington's. The last, Phil Macey, had committed suicide.

Working on a hunch, he decided to check out each of the men's financial records. Bart Yager, the retired cop, had settled down in Columbus in a meager house. There were no signs indicating he had benefited financially, which Parker would have expected if he'd been on the take.

Knowing Grace wouldn't like it but that he had to do it anyway, he checked Frank's resources. The man's daughter had been born with serious physical and mental handicaps, required around-the-clock care and constant medical attention. Frank had insurance but had also suffered a tremendous financial strain over the years, having filed bankruptcy the year before the Gardeners' murder.

So how had he managed to survive and pay the medical bills afterward?

Could Grace be wrong about the man? If he'd been desperate to care for his ill daughter, then maybe he had resorted to taking a bribe or two. Once he had, there would have been no turning back.

If his partner had threatened to expose him, Frank would have gone to jail, then who would have taken care of his daughter? Like any father, he would have wanted to protect her.

But would he have had his own partner killed in order to remain free so he could care for her?

Chapter Fifteen

Grace felt the stilted silence encompassing the room like a thick fog. She wished she and Parker could resort to the easy conversation between them before that heated kiss on the beach.

Heck, she wanted to resume that heated kiss on the beach.

But Parker ate in silence, the troubled look in his eyes warning her that he didn't want to talk. She finished her pasta and carried her plate to the sink, taking a sip of tea to soothe her frayed nerves.

But as he brought his plate to the counter beside her, she gripped the counter edge. "Maybe it's not such a good idea, you staying here."

"I told you I'm not going anywhere until

we catch this guy." He set his plate down. "Then I'll leave and you won't have to deal with me anymore."

That was the trouble. As much as she'd vowed not to get involved with a cop, she had fallen for him.

"Thank you for dinner," he said in a gruff voice.

She angled her head to look at him, thinking ridiculous thoughts—like that she'd enjoy cooking for him every night.

A knock sounded at the door, startling her, and jerking her back to reality. She had to stop torturing herself and fantasizing about a man who would never commit to her.

PARKER JERKED HIS GAZE away from her, then let in the team of officers who'd been searching the beach. "Did you find anything?" he asked.

"We got a partial of a shoe print near that dock," one of the officers said. "I've made a cast of it so we can check for size, shoe treads."

"We also found one bullet casing

lodged in a tree, and another in the sand," the second officer said. "Looks like they belong to a .38."

Like the one used to shoot Bruno and his father. "Good. Any prints on the dock?"

"A couple. We'll see if we can trace them."

He doubted the prints helped, but maybe they'd get lucky. If Juan Carlos had been the shooter, he would have been smart enough to wear gloves. Still, it was worth a shot. "Get it all to forensics, and the bullet to ballistics. If we find Juan Carlos, maybe we'll get a match and we can nail him."

"There's something else," the officer said. "There are signs of breaking and entering next door, so you may have been right. The shooter might have been staying next door."

"Watching Grace," Parker said in a growl.

The officers agreed, then left, and he turned to Grace.

"Pack a bag. We're going to my place."

She frowned. "Are you sure?"

He nodded. For a second before that knock, she'd been getting under his skin again. All during dinner, he'd fought reaching for her hand, kissing her fingertips and telling her how much he liked simply dining with her. How much he liked being in her cozy house, working while she prepared a meal, how he'd like to cook for her sometime, and spend the night.

But not on the couch as he'd do tonight. In her bed.

Knowing the only way to control himself was to keep his distance, he returned to his computer while Grace cleaned up the dishes. "I'm going to shower first, then I'll get my things together."

He nodded, and continued to work so he wouldn't ask her to let him join her.

Yet as the shower water kicked on, he groaned. Closing his eyes, he pictured Grace, beautiful angelic Grace with her flowing long blond hair, naked with water sluicing over her body. He saw the soap bubbles beading on her translucent skin, the water trickling down between her breasts, her nipples rosy and begging for attention, her head thrown back in sublimation.

Frustrated, he stood and paced to the sliding-glass doors. Looked out into the darkness to remind himself that danger lurked outside, that at any moment the killer might return to try to take Grace's life again.

He had to concentrate, focus, and be ready. So when the man came again, he could catch him this time.

And if he laid one hand on Grace, Parker would kill him.

GRACE'S EYES SKIMMED the bare contents of Parker's cabin, noting that he had no personal photos or items that revealed anything about his family. Just books on crime, a boating magazine, furniture that looked masculine and worn.

He insisted she take his bed, and she almost asked him to sleep with her, but held her tongue. She couldn't throw herself at the man. Besides, since the shooting on the beach, he'd been distant, professional, detached.

As she crawled into bed, she inhaled the scent of his body on the pillowcase and her stomach tightened with need.

Knowing that Parker lay in the other room just a few feet away and that she couldn't go to him or touch him drove Grace crazy all night. She finally fell asleep sometime in the early morning hours, only to dream about a killer chasing her down the beach. Then she stumbled over Bruno's body and fell at her parents' dead feet….

She jerked awake, trembling and wondering when the nightmares would end.

Her body ached from fatigue and the abuse it had taken during the car crash. By the time she'd showered and dressed and made it to the kitchen, Parker was freshly shaven and dressed in a blue denim shirt and jeans. The aroma of freshly brewed coffee wafted toward her, and she rummaged through his cabinet, found a cup and poured herself some. Parker had opened the patio doors and was standing outside, a mug in his hand as he stared down the path at the ocean. A hazy cloud cover cast the sky in an ominous gray, and the fall breeze rolling off the ocean made the palm trees sway.

She stepped onto the patio, cradling her coffee between her hands to warm them as a chill cascaded up her spine. "Did you get any sleep?"

He didn't bother to turn around, just kept his broad shoulders stiff, as if to shut her out.

"Some. And you?"

"Some," she said quietly. "So what do we do today?"

It was a loaded question. She wanted to know where they went from here. Wanted him to say that they'd hide out all day, make love and forget the rest of the world existed while they explored each other's body, mind and soul.

He pivoted with a sigh. "I talked to my partner. They tracked down the lab where the hospital obtained the contaminated tissue. Bradford is going to question some of the people at the lab and medical examiner's office today."

Disappointment filled her. He was all business. "Are you going with him?"

He shook his head, then finally looked at her. "He can handle it on his own, and he'll call me and let me know what he finds out." His dark gaze pierced her, as if gauging her reaction to his next statement. "I thought we'd ride over to Columbus this morning."

She blew on her coffee, then took a sip. He'd made the coffee strong, just like him. "What's in Columbus?"

"One of the men who worked with your father years ago. I ran a check last night. Two of the officers who worked with him are dead, one has Huntington's and is in a nursing home, and the other retired to Columbus."

"Do you really think that will do any good, Parker?"

"He might know something about your parents' murder."

She swallowed another sip of coffee, hoping it would renew her waning energy. "I'm sure the police talked to him back then."

Parker shrugged. "Probably. But sometimes after time passes, people remember things differently. If they've lied or withheld information, guilt eats at them and they're ready to confess. That or their reason for lying doesn't exist anymore."

He was still working the dirty cop angle as he had with Frank the night before.

She didn't believe it of Frank, but what if one of the other men who'd worked with her father had been on the take? If her father had found out and threatened to come forward, the cop might have been desperate enough to kill her family.

And after all these years of getting away with murder, it would be reason enough to silence Bruno.

THE RIDE to Columbus was virtually silent. Parker understood Grace's hesitancy to question her father's coworkers, men who might have been his close friends, but if he was going to find out the truth about who killed the Gardeners, he had to probe into the past and that meant Jim Gardner's relationships at work. If anyone knew about Gardener's enemies, it would be his fellow officers.

And Frank Johnson obviously wasn't talking.

He studied the small ranch house in the subdivision on the outskirts of Columbus. Not very big, no fancy car, no visible signs of money indicating the man had been on the take.

He parked and climbed out, then circled in front of the car to help Grace, but she waved off his help. She was obviously still hurt over his comment the night before.

How would she feel if he wound up having to arrest Frank?

"I really think this is a waste of time," Grace said as he rang the doorbell.

Parker gave her a noncommittal look. "It's part of the job, questioning everybody related to a victim."

She lowered her gaze to her hands where she twisted them together. The door sprang open and a gray-haired, pudgy woman stood, leaning on a horse head cane. "Yes?"

"Mrs. Yager?" Parker asked.

"Yes. What can I do for you?"

"My name is Detective Kilpatrick from the S.P.D., and this is Grace Gardener."

Mrs. Yager pursed her lips. "Gardener? That name sounds familiar."

"My father, Jim Gardner, worked with your husband," Grace explained.

"Oh, yes, oh, my." She clapped her hands over her cheeks. "Little Grace Gardener, it's been such a long time, and you're all grown up now."

Grace gave him an awkward look, and Parker wanted to comfort her, but managed to contain himself. "Can we talk to your husband?"

"Of course." She waved them in, then toward the back. "He's in the garden outside. I'll get some sweet iced-tea and bring it out."

Parker thanked her, and he and Grace made their way through the tiny, cluttered kitchen to the patio.

Bart Yager was craggy-looking with a rounded belly and sweat-stained shirt. He stood, narrowing his eyes as they approached.

Parker explained the reason for their visit, and for a moment, Bart's face turned chalky-white as if he'd seen a ghost.

"Good gracious alive, child. You look like your mother."

Grace bit down on her lip, and Parker slid a hand to her back this time. She tensed, then took a seat on the metal glider while Bart removed a handkerchief, wiped at his face and hands, then met his wife to help her outside with the refreshments.

Parker waited until she'd disappeared back inside the house before addressing the older man. "We appreciate your time, Mr. Yager. I don't know if you heard that Grace's brother Bruno was recently killed."

The old man slurped down half his glass of tea. "Yes, I was sorry to hear about that. Poor boy."

"We don't believe it was suicide," Grace interjected. "Someone killed him."

"Really?" The old man made a weary sound.

Parker explained about the murder attempts on Grace. "We think that one of Bruno's cases got him killed."

A long silence. "What was he working on?"

"We've ruled out a couple of them, but he was definitely investigating his parents' murder."

"Geesh, that boy never could let it go," Bart mumbled.

"Why should we?" Grace asked. "Their killer was never caught."

Bart reached out a hand and covered Grace's. "I'm sorry. I didn't mean it like that. I just hate to see you two live in the past."

"How can I not?" Grace asked. "Especially when Bruno was killed over it, and the killer is still free."

"He also might be after Grace," Parker said in a cold voice.

"Tell us what happened back then, Bart. Do you know who killed my parents?" Grace asked.

"No. God, no." Bart's breathing turned labored. "If I had, I would have arrested him myself. Your father and I were friends."

"Bruno may have uncovered the fact that one of the cops on the force with Jim Gardener was dirty."

Bart stood with a pained grunt, his knees popping. "What are you implying?"

"I'm not implying anything," Parker said. "I think Frank Johnson may have been taking bribes, and Jim found out so he had him killed."

Grace gasped and Bart glared at him.

"If it wasn't Frank," Parker continued, lowering his voice a decibel, "then it was one of you. Don't you think enough people have died to keep this secret, that it's time to tell the truth?"

BART'S WIFE GASPED and Grace winced at the stricken look in her eyes. Apparently she'd walked outside in time to overhear enough of their conversation to understand Parker's implications.

Bart went to her and curved his arm around her waist. "I think you'd best go now, Detective."

Grace gave him an apologetic look. This

man had been one of her father's friends, just as Frank had. And from everything Bruno had told her, most of the guys who worked on the force considered themselves brothers.

They would die for one another.

Did that mean that they would also lie to cover up illegal activities?

Surely not if it meant letting a killer go free....

"Secrets have a way of coming out," Parker said in a low but lethal voice.

"I told you everything I know," Bart snapped. "Now please leave. You're upsetting my wife."

Parker stepped toward Bart, but Grace clutched his arm. "Please, Parker, let's leave."

He stiffened. "We'll go for now, Mr. Yager, but I will get to the bottom of this. So if you decide to talk, let me know."

"I'm sorry," Grace murmured, then she turned and followed Parker outside. Even with his limp, he was walking so fast she could barely keep up with him.

When they reached the car, he spun toward her. "You don't have to apologize to them for me, Grace. I'm doing my job and Bart Yager knows it."

"But, Parker—"

"Don't you understand?" he said through gritted teeth. "Your brother was murdered and you might be next. And the killer may be someone you trust."

Grace shook her head, disbelief pummeling her. Parker had to be wrong. She had so few people in her life that she trusted—she couldn't bear to think that one of them had betrayed her and her brother.

HELLFIRE and damnation. Bruno Gardener's body had been exhumed. The medical examiner was going to reexamine his remains.

Then they would find the truth.

The truth he had worked so hard to keep hidden.

Detective Kilpatrick and Bruno's sister were getting way too close to everything.

It was time for them to be extinguished.

He followed them back to Kilpatrick's, then waited patiently until they disappeared inside.

Then he punched in Kilpatrick's number.

Like a good cop, he answered on the second ring. "Kilpatrick."

"This is an old friend of Jim Gardener's. I heard you've been asking questions."

"Yes."

"If you want the truth, meet me at Serpent's Cove."

"Why don't you tell me what you need to right now?"

"It's too dangerous." He hesitated, driving home his point. "And you'd better come alone."

He disconnected the call and watched, breathing a sigh of relief when Kilpatrick exited the cottage without Grace. He'd fallen for the trap.

Laugher bubbled in his throat. But neither he nor Grace Gardener was safe. First, he'd take care of Grace. After all, she would be the easiest to dispose of.

Then he'd finish off the detective. And once again prove he was invincible and smarter than the cops.

Chapter Sixteen

Parker didn't want to leave Grace alone for a second, but he didn't trust the man who'd called. He might be walking into a trap.

And he refused to take her into it with him.

She would be safer here alone.

But still, he'd left her with an extra firearm and ordered her to lock all the doors. As he drove away from the cottage, he phoned Bradford, explained about the call and asked him to send a uniform by to check on Grace while he was gone.

"You want me to meet you?" Bradford asked.

"No, I can handle this. I don't want to scare him off in case he's legit."

"When you finish, swing by the ME's

office. He's doing Bruno's autopsy now. We might have news on him soon."

"I'll go back and get Grace first. She'll want to be there, too." His gut tightened. "Besides, I really don't want to leave her alone for long."

"She knows how to use the piece you left with her?"

"Yeah." But he didn't know if Grace would actually use it—she'd spent her life healing the sick, not taking lives. But hopefully if she needed to defend herself, she would.

"Walsh, see if you can pull Frank Johnson and Bart Yager's phone records. I'd like to know if either one of them has been in contact with Juan Carlos. And check Juan's visitation log when he was in prison. Maybe that will lead us to who hired him."

"Good idea, I'll get right on it." Bradford paused. "By the way, I questioned one of the guys from that body-moving service. He led me back to L-Tech."

"And?"

"I paid them a visit. One of the lab techs, a guy named Sonny Pradham, admitted that he screwed up in storing some of the tissue they received."

"So it was just a mistake by one of the lab workers?"

"It looks that way. The lab has also been tracking down all the tissue that might have been contaminated and recalling it."

"But this guy will lose his job," Parker said.

"Yeah, and there will be lawsuits through the roof. And with the deaths associated with the problematic tissue, the DA is contemplating criminal charges for negligent homicide. This bastard's stupid mistake has affected a lot of lives and he's probably going to do some time."

Parker flexed his leg. Even scarred and with more therapy to go, he was grateful to be alive.

Grace's face flashed into his mind.

Now he had to keep her that way, too.

Maybe tonight he'd get the answers she wanted about her family's deaths and he could put the killer in jail.

Then she could move on with her life.

Only he wouldn't be in it.

His chest squeezed and he rolled down the window, needing air.

It didn't matter if he'd be with her or not. Grace would be safe; she could have the happiness a woman like her should have. The family and love she deserved. A life not tainted by violence or crime.

One that a jaded, scarred cop could never give her.

GRACE WAS wound tight. Parker had been nervous about leaving her, and she'd wanted to go with him, but he'd insisted it was too dangerous.

Who had called him so mysteriously? What did the man have to tell him that he couldn't have relayed over the phone? Why hadn't he asked to meet at the police station?

What if Parker got hurt?

The familiar terror she'd experienced since her brother had joined the police force nagged at her. Each time her father or Bruno had left for work, she'd known it might be the last time she'd see them alive.

She couldn't suffer that terrible anxiety again.

Yet she'd fallen for Parker anyway.

Even as she tried to harden her heart now, she knew it was futile. She was in love with the man, cop and all.

Wanting to know more about him, she walked through his den, searching for photos of him and any family he might have. He'd told her they were gone, but again found no personal photos of anyone in the house. A fitness magazine along with several books on forensics lay on the oak coffee table, yet his cabin was free of decoration or color, everything was done in neutrals as if he hadn't given a thought to decor. So like a man.

But it revealed a lot about him. He was fairly neat, clean, organized.

Detached. He didn't keep clutter or anything personal around because he was a loner. A man who had no commitments or relationships.

Because he didn't want them….

Like her brother, he was married to the job.

Unsettled by the thought, she paced to the sliding-glass doors and stared out into the cool, gray evening. Beyond the trees, the ocean pounded at high tide. Waves crashed and broke, beating fiercely just like her heart.

How could she have allowed herself to fall in love with a man so like the men she'd grown up with? The ones who'd left her….

The wind whistled through the trees, the palms swayed and a clap of thunder rent the air. Something clattered and, behind her, from the storage room off the kitchen, glass shattered.

The lights suddenly flickered off.

A cold wave of fear shot through her. She spun around and raced toward the kitchen drawer where Parker had left a pistol for her. She'd promised him she'd use it if needed, but her hands shook as she fumbled past the small oak table. Her hip hit the edge of the breakfast bar and she yelped in pain, knocking the phone book to the floor with a thud.

A footstep creaked in the darkness, then the sound of someone's breathing echoed in her ear. Oh, God, someone was in the house.

Her pulse raced as she lunged toward the drawer, but just as she caught the edge, the man grabbed her around the neck and jerked her against him. The scent of sweat, salt and cigarette smoke assaulted her. She clawed wildly, scrambling for something to protect herself with, and her hand connected with one of the kitchen knives. She jerked it up and stabbed backward, hoping to connect with flesh.

He slapped her, making her ears ring. "Damn it, you bitch!"

She swung the knife again, but his hands tightened around her throat and her lungs begged for air. The knife must have pierced his thigh because he yowled in pain, but the blow angered him more and he slammed his fist into the side of her head.

The knife clattered to the floor and the room spun in a sickening cloud of black.

She slid downward, unable to breathe as he yanked her toward the door.

Outside, clamshells sliced her bare legs as he dragged her across the drive, then he picked her up like a rag doll and tossed her into the trunk. Nausea and terror clogged her throat and she screamed, but the sound died as he slammed the trunk shut.

PARKER PULLED his car into Serpent's Cove and parked, his senses alert. He didn't see another car anywhere nearby, and hadn't spotted one on the dirt road that led to the cove. The place was virtually deserted, but sounds could go undetected, lost in the wind whistling off the ocean and the waves roaring over the jagged rocks. Rocks that created snakelike shapes along the wall of the ledge and climbed from the beach like a small mountain carved toward the heavens.

A dangerous place, one that had taken more than one life from a fall.

Had the caller really intended to meet him and give him information, or had he lured him here to push him over the edge?

Parker searched the beach below in case the man was waiting beneath the ledge, but saw nothing but water washing away sand and tossing shells and driftwood onto the shore.

Clouds rumbled above, casting a shadow over the moon and hinting at a storm on the rise. Something crackled behind him and he spun around, expecting to see someone approaching, but a beer can caught in the wind rolled across the rocks, then tumbled over the ledge.

Frustrated, he paced along the cove for the next ten minutes, checking the beach below, his watch, the shadows of the trees lining the road. Impatience gnawed at him, along with the nagging feeling that the call could have been a trap to lure him away from Grace.

His heart pounding, he unpocketed his cell phone and punched in his home number. He didn't like being away from her, had to make sure she was safe.

Continuing to track the area for the mysterious caller, he paced the cove. The phone rang several times, but no answer.

The machine finally clicked on. "Grace, if you're there, please pick up. I need to know you're okay."

She didn't respond. Panic teased at him, but he assured himself she might have taken a shower or fallen asleep. Still, he punched in her cell phone number, yet as it rang and rang, the bad premonition tugging at him echoed louder in his mind.

Something was wrong.

He dialed the precinct and asked for the local who was supposed to drive by to check on Grace. A minute later dispatch connected him to a uniform named Brewster.

"This is Detective Kilpatrick. Have you checked on Grace Gardener at my place?"

"I'm pulling down your street now."

"Good, I just called her and she didn't answer, so knock, then if you don't get an answer, go on in. But be sure to identify yourself and be careful—I left her with one of my pieces."

"Got it."

Parker gripped the phone tighter and

twisted to scan the road again. "I'll hold while you check."

The next five minutes stretched into an eternity as Parker listened to Brewster knock on the door. The man pounded hard, then shouted his name and identified himself.

Parker prayed she would answer the door and he'd know she was all right.

"Miss Gardener!" Brewster shouted again.

Parker paced, his instincts roaring to life, shouting that something was wrong.

"She's not responding," Brewster said into the phone. "I'm going to check the windows and doors now."

Parker held his breath, then a second later Brewster muttered, "Looks like a window was bashed in your laundry room. And the lights are out."

"Damn it to hell." Parker scraped a hand over his jaw. "Get inside now! Find out if Grace is there."

Parker heard Brewster kick the door, then his boots clattering on the floor. Sweat poured down his face as Parker ran for his car, jumped inside and clicked on the engine. He tore away from the cove, cursing himself that he'd fallen for a trap.

"She's not here, no one is," Brewster shouted into the phone. "But there are signs of a struggle and blood on the kitchen counter."

Emotions choked Parker. He prayed he wouldn't be too late, that Grace wasn't already dead.

GRACE STRUGGLED to regain control as the car bumped along the road. The trunk was suffocating, hot and smelled of grease. Her head throbbed, her hair was glued to her scalp and she felt blood dripping into the tangled strands.

But she would not give up hope.

She had to fight for her life, find a way to stall this man from killing her long enough for Parker to track her down.

And he would find her; she had to believe that. He was probably already looking for her, on this man's trail now.

Unless the call had been a trap and the killer had gotten to Parker first.

Panic robbed her breath, but she forced the dismal thoughts at bay. She wouldn't accept that Parker was dead.

But hadn't her family, her brother, all deserted her when she thought they were invincible, as well?

Grateful her attacker hadn't bound her hands, she searched frantically for an inside latch to the trunk. If she could pop it open, maybe she could get out. But would she jump with the car moving?

Yes. If it was the only way to escape, she'd do it.

Her fingers fumbled clumsily, something sharp jabbing at her side, and she shivered as a bug crawled down her arm. She shook it off, knowing it was nothing compared to what the man who'd grabbed her would do to her when he stopped. Hissing between clenched teeth as the car hit a pothole and her body bounced painfully into a hard object that might have been a jack, she dug her nails into the flooring to steady herself. Finally, just as the car slowed, her fingers found the lock.

Before she could pop the trunk, the car

screeched to a halt. She fumbled with the lock, desperate, trying to hurry, but suddenly the top flipped up and a shadow lurked above her, daunting as he waved a gun in her face.

"You should have taken the earlier warnings," he muttered in a husky voice.

"Who are you? Why are you doing this to me?" she asked.

He reached for her arm and she kicked him in the chest, but he jerked her up by the hair and jammed the gun against her head. "Try that again and your brain will be splattered all over this dock for your boyfriend to find."

She froze, her heart slamming into her ribs. At least she knew now that Parker was still alive.

So why had he brought her to the dock? Was he taking her out on a boat?

Was he going to kill her or not?

He dragged her from the car, and she squinted to see his face. He had brown skin, thick eyebrows, was Hispanic. Juan Carlos, the man Parker had been hunting for?

A paid killer.

"Who hired you to do this?" she asked, determined once and for all to unearth the truth.

A litany of Spanish followed, then he tossed her onto a small fishing boat. She tried to brace her fall, but her body slammed against the wood and she cried out as her ankle twisted beneath her.

"Where are you taking me?" she cried.

He waved the gun at her again. "You ask too many questions, *señorita*."

"Tell me who hired you," she demanded.

"You really want to know? You should have asked your father's partner."

No, not Frank. Anger made her jump up and lunge toward him. "You're lying. Frank wouldn't hurt me, he loves me—"

He hit her with the butt of the gun and sent her body flailing back. She frantically clawed for control, but her hands connected only with air, and the blow made her ears ring and the world spin. Before she could regain her balance, he grabbed her hands and tied them together, then secured her feet. She kicked at him and struggled to fight back, but another blow knocked her onto the floor of the boat and the next time she opened her eyes, he was clutching a couple of bricks.

Oh, God, he was going to tie them to her feet and dump her in the ocean for the sharks to devour.

She lifted her bound hands and felt for the St. Christopher medal, but it was gone, just like Bruno. She must have lost it in her house during the attack. Or maybe in the car. A sob wrenched her. It was the last thing she'd had of her family's and now it was gone, too.

For some insane reason, she thought of the date. October 30, the day before Halloween. Kids were home, excitedly getting their costumes ready; spooks and goblins and fairies and princesses. People were buying candy to prepare for the trick-or-treaters. Others would be having parties, bobbing for apples, making haunted houses, lighting jack-o'-lanterns that would glow in the dark.

Tonight storms brewed in the sky.

Clouds covered the moon, obliterating the light. Other people were walking on the beach hand-in-hand, sharing a romantic night. Living normal lives. Planning their futures, thinking of names for the babies they would have. Others sat in rocking chairs on the sleeping porches, growing old together as their grandchildren chased fireflies in the yard.

She would never take a romantic walk on the beach or have children or make scrapbooks of her grandchildren.

Today was the day she would die.

Chapter Seventeen

Parker spotted the blood smeared against the kitchen counter and a cold knot of fear gripped him. Grace could not be dead.

Further scrutiny assured him that the blood loss wasn't substantial, and he breathed a sigh of relief, although he knew good and damn well that she wasn't out of the danger zone.

The killer had her.

Why hadn't he finished her off here?

The possibilities made his gut twist. Because he didn't intend to kill her, only scare her?

No, he'd already murdered. His violence would only escalate.

The truth nipped at his conscience—the man didn't want to leave her body behind.

Doing so meant leaving evidence that might be traced back to him.

Something sparkled in the dark interior of the room and he knelt, then realized it was Grace's St. Christopher's medal. She must have lost it in the struggle.

He used a handkerchief to pick it up, then bagged it. "Get the crime scene team out here now," he told Brewster. "And make sure they check this necklace for prints or trace. Grace always wore it. The killer might have touched it when he grabbed her."

Brewster nodded and phoned for a team while Parker called Bradford. His head spun with worry, panic jumbling his thoughts. He needed help.

"They've got Grace," he said without preamble. "Hell, Walsh, we have to do something. Figure out where he might take her."

"We will. We've still got the gang in custody, so it's not them."

"No, this is bigger than they are."

"You just came from Yager's when you received the call?"

"Right."

"I'll send an officer to his place to see what he knows." A pause and voices echoed in the room, then Bradford cleared his throat. "Listen, Parker, come to the station. Roundtree is here and says he has to talk to you."

"Can it wait?"

"I told him Grace is missing and he says it has to do with her and Bruno."

"I'll be right there."

He hung up and dashed toward his car at a dead run. Sweat rolled down his jaw as he wheeled from the driveway and sped toward Savannah. He honked at a moving truck and raced around the slower cars, siren blaring. It was the night before Halloween, a Friday night, and traffic was thick as locals left work and headed to happy hour.

He met a fire truck roaring toward Skidaway and grimaced, but someone else would take that call. Tonight he had to save Grace.

Precious minutes lapsed while he hit a snag maneuvering around a biker trio, but he finally made it to the precinct and hurried inside.

"Where's Walsh and Roundtree?" he asked as he entered the bullpen.

An officer gestured toward the back. "In Captain Black's office."

He raced toward the office and pounded on the door. A minute later his stomach clenched at the grim expression on Black's face.

"Sit down, Roundtree has something to show you," the captain said.

Parker crossed his arms. "I'm fine standing."

Roundtree was sweating profusely as he clutched an envelope between his hands. "I should have come forward sooner, but...they threatened my family, my wife, my baby girl...."

Emotions made the man's voice break and Parker didn't doubt for a minute that Roundtree was telling the truth. Still, if he'd endangered Grace...

"Just spill it," Parker barked.

Roundtree scrubbed his hand over his neck with a pained look. "Bruno sent this to me. It came after he died with a note that said I was to turn it over to the captain if something happened to him."

"But you waited?" Parker asked in a clipped tone.

Roundtree dropped his head into his hands, his expression tortured. "I told you they threatened my family."

"Who threatened you?" the captain asked before Parker could grind out the question.

"I don't know." Roundtree's voice cracked. "It was anonymous, but I knew it was real. There were photos of my wife and baby inside—the photos were chopped in a dozen pieces."

"Damn," Bradford muttered.

Parker bit back a reply, but instead gestured toward the envelope. "What's inside?"

Roundtree shoved the envelope toward him. "Information that connects Frank Johnson, Bart Yager and another cop they worked with to the Gardeners' murders."

Parker muttered a curse. "We have to bring in Johnson and Yager."

"I've sent a local to get Yager," Captain Black said. "And I put a call in to Johnson, but he's not at home. His housekeeper said his daughter took a turn for the worse and he's at Savannah General with her now."

Parker fisted his hands by his sides. "Is there anything else I should know?"

"There are notes on financial records, proof that McKendrick, Yager and Johnson were on the take," Roundtree said. "And information that leads the men to Juan Carlos. We checked the visitor's log and Yager visited him twice in the past year."

Parker backed toward the door. "I'm going to talk to Frank, see if he knows where Juan Carlos would take Grace."

"I'll go with you," Bradford said.

"Check back." Captain Black waved them to go. "I'll let you know if we hear from Yager."

Bradford and Parker hurried toward Parker's car. Parker jumped in and they sped away.

If Frank Johnson cared for Grace at all and had something to do with her disappearance, he'd have to talk now.

Parker would beat the truth out of him if he had to.

EVEN WITH the siren blaring, maneuvering around the Friday-night crowd in Savannah proved to be a bitch. Parker almost skidded into a telephone pole as he rounded a corner and sped through a red light, honking his horn to keep the pedestrians and cars who refused to give way to emergency vehicles ample warning that he was plowing through. Every second counted.

He'd take them with him if he had to in order to save Grace.

He careened into the parking lot, screeching to a stop near the emergency room entrance, then vaulted from the car. Bradford jogged on his heels, the two of them racing against time.

He ran straight for the nurses' station. "Detectives Kilpatrick and Walsh. We need to speak to Frank Johnson, he brought his daughter in."

The nurse wrinkled her nose then checked the computer screen. "Yes, she's not doing well, is in ICU now. He's probably in the waiting room—"

Parker cut her off. "What floor?"

"Third—"

He didn't wait for her to elaborate, or for the elevator. He ran for the stairs. Bradford rushed behind him.

When they cleared the landing, he shoved open the door and glanced at the signs.

"Waiting room's to the left," Bradford said, and Parker took off.

He rushed down the corridor and around the turn, then spotted Johnson sitting in one of the waiting room chairs, leaning over with his elbows on his knees, his hands cradling his head. His body shook with emotions, indicating that his daughter's condition wasn't good. Bradford caught his arm and gave him an odd look, compassion for Johnson in his eyes. But a second later the realization of what they had to do registered.

Anger drove Parker toward the man. Grace's life hung in the balance the same as this man's daughter's might. When

Parker stopped in front of him, Johnson heaved a deep breath, then slowly lifted his gaze.

"She's not going to make it," Frank said in a tortured voice.

For a brief second Parker's breath halted in his chest. Was he talking about Grace?

"Kelly…" Frank whispered. "She has pneumonia now. Doc says she may go any minute."

Parker's chest squeezed. "I'm sorry, Frank."

Frank nodded, his breathing heavy as tears rolled down his ruddy cheeks. "I don't know how I'll go on."

Bradford cleared his throat and Parker claimed a seat beside Frank. "I know it's hard and this is a terrible time, Frank," Parker said, "but Grace is missing. Someone abducted her from my house."

Frank's alarmed gaze shot to him. "Dear God, I tried to convince her to quit poking around."

"It's too late for that," Parker snapped. "Bruno's partner, Roundtree, gave us a file. It has information he'd gathered about you and Yager and one of your fellow officers—"

"McKendrick. He has Huntington's now."

"What happened, Frank?" Bradford asked quietly.

"It was a long damn time ago. We were all young, broke, eager…then my wife had Kelly and died…" A sound of remorse tore from his gut and Parker patted him on the back.

"One of you hired Juan Carlos to kill Grace?" Parker asked.

"Yager. Just wanted to scare her, not kill her."

"We think he may have her now. I questioned Yager earlier. He may have panicked," Parker rasped. "If Carlos has Grace, where the hell would he take her?"

Frank wiped at his eyes. "I don't know."

Parker ground his fist into the chair edge. "Think, Johnson, think. Grace's life depends on us finding her."

Frank blew out a breath. "The marina. Yager left his payment in a locker at the boathouse. Check there."

Parker nodded, and stood while Bradford remained seated. "Go ahead, Parker, I'll wait here in case he thinks of anything else."

Frank gave him a somber look. "If you're worried about me skipping out, don't. I'll be right here with Kelly until she's gone."

"And then what?" Parker asked.

"If you haven't found Grace by then, I'll be on the streets helping you find her." He threaded his hands together. "Anyways, I'm not running out on my daughter or Grace. If they both die, there's nothing for me to live for anyway."

Anguish darkened Frank's tone and eyes, and Parker nodded, hearing the truth and despair in his words. For a moment he actually sympathized with the man.

If Grace died, he didn't know if he'd want to live, either.

GRACE SQUIRMED and twisted her fingers and hands, struggling to loosen the ropes around her wrists, but the hemp cut into her skin and wouldn't budge. The heavy pull of the bricks against her arms and feet made her ache and filled her with despair.

"Please, don't do this," Grace pleaded.

"Shut up. You had fair warning," Carlos growled.

"They'll find you," Grace shouted. "Parker will hunt you down and take you back to jail."

Carlos laughed in her face, his rancid breath beating at her cheeks. "I'll never go back to jail. And, sweetheart, your boyfriend is going to die just like you are."

"No!" Grace screamed, hoping someone nearby might hear, but her voice died in the breeze off the ocean, and from what she could detect in the dark, the dock appeared to be deserted.

Carlos secured her ropes again, then popped open a beer and drank greedily. She watched him, hatred suffusing her. He had killed Bruno and now he would kill her.

But betrayal sank in, cutting deeper. He hadn't killed her parents—Frank, the man she trusted with her life, the man who'd been family to her, had been responsible. All the times Frank had visited and taken Bruno fishing. The day he'd attended Doughnuts for Dads with her, proudly calling her his second daughter.

The holidays he'd shared Thanksgiving dinner with her and Bruno flashed back. The Christmases they'd spent with him and Kelly. The bike he'd bought for her seventh birthday; the way he'd run along behind her holding it so she wouldn't fall. His deep voice echoing that he would catch her if she did, that he wouldn't let anything hurt her….

Tears choked her throat and clogged her eyes, running down her face, but she was helpless to wipe them away with the weights tied to her arms. How could Frank have lived with himself? How could he have let her parents be murdered, knowing she and Bruno would be parentless?

Did Frank know that Carlos had her now? Would he help her if he did, or would he let her die like he had her parents and brother?

PARKER THREW THE CAR into park and jumped out at the marina, his gaze frantically searching the parking lot for cars. The place was virtually deserted tonight, except for an old battered truck parked at one end and a rusted green Chevy at the opposite.

"I'll check out the pickup, and inside the shack for lockers," Bradford said in a whisper.

"I'll take the Chevy."

Bradford inched to the right and crouched down as he wove behind posts and an old fishing shack. Parker inched down the dock, his gun braced between his hands as he scoped out the distance of the dock and quickly scanned each slip he passed for signs of movement. He passed a couple of nice sailboats, then a houseboat, but both were dark and deserted. Further down, he spotted a motorized fishing boat, then a smaller wooden one. But as he neared, the engine sounded and suddenly the motorboat eased off across the inlet.

It had to be Carlos. And he was getting away with Grace.

Was she still alive? Would he dump her in the ocean?

Hell, no…Parker had to stop him.

He jumped into the other fishing boat. It took him precious seconds to hotwire the engine but finally it kicked into action and he shot into the inlet to give chase. Salt water sprayed his face as he sped up, bouncing over the waves created in the wake of the other boat. He accelerated, closing the distance, and saw Carlos standing at the wheel, racing ahead.

His lungs tightened. Where was Grace?

Carlos glanced over his shoulder, spotted Parker and fired over his shoulder, but Parker spun the boat sideways to dodge the shot and the bullet was lost in the wind. Rage fueled Parker's determination, and he accelerated another notch, tasting salt as the waves sprayed his face. Above, thunder boomed. A rain cloud opened up and rain pelted down.

He hit another wave and bounced, but closed the distance to Carlos's boat, then

Carlos veered a sharp right and raced toward the open sea.

Parker battled panic. If he made it too far out and lost him, he'd never save Grace.

The sound of another boat cut through the noise and he angled his head to see Bradford approaching. Relief at having backup bolstered his courage and he veered toward the right to chase Carlos. A minute later he zoomed up on his tail.

Carlos fired at him, then slowed, and Parker watched in horror as the man lifted Grace from the boat. She fought him, but he'd tied bricks to her hands and feet, then he tossed her into the ocean.

Her scream echoed in the wind as she sank under.

Parker slammed his boat to a halt. He could go after Carlos or Grace.

There was no question. He dove into the churning waters.

Chapter Eighteen

Parker fought the current as he ducked below the surface, desperately searching for Grace. He spotted her and his heart spasmed.

Though she was fighting the undertow, the bricks weighed her down and she sank deeper and deeper into the water. He swam toward her, battling his way through the current trying to sweep him out to sea. His lungs begged for air, and his eyes stung, his leg muscles protesting the waves, but he finally made it to Grace.

Her eyes widened in a plea, and thankfully she was still holding her breath, but time meant everything. He grabbed her around the shoulders and dragged her upward. The weights made her so heavy that with the current he barely climbed to the surface. They both came up gasping, but caught a breath before the waves sucked them back down.

Fortified by that breath, he ducked deeper to untie her feet. The ropes were tight around her ankles, swollen from the water, and he jerked a knife from his pocket and cut through them, letting the bricks sink. The ropes at her wrists came next, but her face looked panic-stricken, and she needed air. A second later he finally freed her from the weights, then grabbed her and swam upward, breaking the surface again. She cried out raggedly and inhaled a breath, while he caught one, too, then he swam toward the shore, carrying her with him.

The beach seemed miles away, but the sound of an engine broke through the noise of the crashing waves, and he squinted through the rain and saw the boat approaching. Was Carlos coming back?

He treaded water as the boat approached, and shouted in relief when he saw Bradford at the wheel. His partner swung the boat to the right, then coasted toward them. Parker swam to the edge, taking Grace with him and guiding her in front of him so Bradford could help her inside the boat.

"Where's Carlos?" Parker shouted.

"Dead," Bradford muttered as he offered a hand to Parker. "He crashed into an embankment trying to escape. I've already called it in."

Parker glanced back and saw flames bursting toward the sky. Thank God the man was gone. Then he dropped down beside Grace, panting from exertion.

"Parker…" She gulped for air, spitting out water, crying and shaking from the trauma. Five minutes later and he would have been too late.

His muscles ached from the strain and his leg immediately stiffened, but he forgot the pain as he dragged her into his arms and held her.

GRACE TREMBLED all over, the past hour crashing back like snippets from a nightmare. Carlos kidnapping her, weighing her down with those bricks, trying to drown her....

But Parker had saved her. She had to hang on to that reality.

She clung to him, grateful to be alive, sobbing as he rocked her in his arms.

"It's okay now, Grace. Shh." He cradled her against his chest, stroking her back, her hair, his voice a mere whisper in her ear as he consoled her. Wind and rain pummeled them, but he shielded her with his body as his partner steered the boat toward the inlet and into the dock.

"Frank..." she said brokenly. "He and Yager and another man...they had my parents killed."

He stroked her hair. "I know, baby, we've talked to Frank, and the cops are picking up Yager. The third guy is in the hospital with Huntington's disease. I'm so sorry."

"I can't believe it," she said, then broke into more gut-wrenching cries.

He cradled her to him, letting her purge her anguish. "What will happen to Frank?" she whispered hoarsely.

"We'll question him, take him into custody. They'll probably serve time for murder."

Another sob escaped her. "But Kelly, his daughter, she needs him…"

He tensed. "I'm sorry, Grace, but she's at the hospital. They don't expect her to live through the night."

Sorrow mingled with her anger. Frank loved his daughter more than life itself, had done all of it for her. And now Kelly would be gone and Frank would go to jail.

And she had no one left.

She shivered as the boat slowed to a stop, then Bradford climbed out first. Parker helped her to stand and Bradford helped her onto the dock, then Parker jumped out behind her. Once again, he cradled her in his arms and guided her toward his car.

"I'll wait here for the authorities to retrieve Carlos's body," Bradford said.

An ambulance screeched to a halt and two medics jumped out and hurried toward them.

"Check her out," Parker said, leading Grace to the ambulance.

One of the EMTs began taking her vitals while the other handed her a blanket.

"How about you, sir?" the medic asked.

"I'm all right," Parker said. "Just make sure she is."

Parker stepped aside to talk to Bradford while the medics examined her, and she winced as they treated the gash on her head. But the entire time they checked her, she kept looking at Parker, thinking how much she wanted to be near him, how she'd almost died tonight and she didn't want to spend the rest of the evening alone.

"We suggested she go to the hospital, but she refused," one of the medics told Parker.

"I don't need to go to the hospital," Grace said, although her voice still sounded shaky.

"Grace—"

"Please, Parker, I just want to go home, take a warm bath and rest, forget that this night happened."

Parker nodded in concession. "We'll

need a formal statement, but you can do that tomorrow."

She gripped his arm to steady herself as she rose from the gurney. "Fine, just not tonight."

The medics insisted she sign a form stating that she refused hospital treatment, then left, and Parker informed Bradford that he was taking her home.

When they reached the car, he halted by the door and looked down into her eyes, his expression tender and concerned. "Are you sure you're all right, Grace? You look so pale, and those bruises look pretty bad."

"I'm all right, Parker. Please, just take me home."

His eyes flickered with worry, but also with other emotions. Concern. Affection. Desire.

Then he climbed in the car, started the engine and drove toward his house. She clutched his hand, her heart racing as they neared his cabin. She'd lied when she said she just wanted a warm bath and rest.

She wanted a night in Parker's arms. In his bed.

A night of him loving her, one without cops or killers or questions.

A night of pretending they could be together forever, that he wouldn't leave her as everyone else in her life had.

GRACE HAD been through a terrible ordeal. She looked fragile and delicate, as though she might break apart any second.

But even drenched in sea water with her hair a tangled mess, she was so damn beautiful that when she turned those needy eyes toward him, pure raw hunger shot through Parker, setting him ablaze.

He'd almost lost her tonight.

The mere thought brought a surge of panic again, and his hand tightened around the steering wheel. Thank God Carlos was dead and she was safe.

Emotions bombarded him as he parked, and they ran through the drizzling rain up to his cabin door. Grace shivered against him, and he pulled her into the crook of his arms and led her to the shower.

"Bath or shower?" he asked.

"Shower," she said softly, then reached for his hand.

He hesitated, narrowing his eyes to study her, wanting to make sure he understood her silent request.

"Please, Parker, you're cold, too."

Her soft-whispered plea shattered any lingering reservations he had. Then she reached up and began to unbutton his shirt and he wasn't cold at all, but so hot he thought he might combust. One by one she unfastened the buttons until his shirt lay open and she pushed it over his shoulders.

He touched her cheek, gently, moved by the fierce hunger in her eyes. No woman had ever looked at him with such desire.

But he was a scarred man.

His jaw tightened and he caught her hand in his. "It's not pretty," he said in a guttural voice.

The sweetest smile touched her mouth. "Don't you know how much I want you, Parker? Nothing matters except being together."

His heartbeat accelerated, pounding in his chest. "I want you, too, Grace. I have ever since you brought me back to life in the ER."

A shudder tore through her, and he realized she was still cold. Or maybe trembling from her battle in the water against those weights. Carlos had been a sick, sadistic bastard.

He wanted to show her another kind of man.

Make her forget that Frank, the man she'd trusted all her life, had betrayed her, and now everyone she'd ever loved was gone.

He flipped on the shower water to let it warm, then began to undress her slowly, peeling away her clothes to reveal her slender body. Anger knotted his stomach at the bruises on her wrists and body, and he clenched his jaw, but she pressed a hand to his cheek, then kissed him tenderly.

"Make me forget tonight," she whispered. "Please, Parker, let's both forget."

She didn't know what she was asking.

He lived his life dealing in pain and anger, not pleasure. But tonight he vowed to give her that gift.

And to give it to himself.

She slid her clothes to the floor and stepped out of them, and stood only in a pale pink bra and matching lace bikini panties. She was so strong yet so soft. So utterly feminine that his sex hardened and begged for her touch.

As if she'd read his mind, he claimed her mouth with his, kissing her while his hands worked at her bra. The garment fell at her feet, then she stepped out of her panties, and his body surged with need. His tongue danced with hers while she unfastened his jeans. At the sound of his zipper rasping, he thought he might explode. He pulled his mouth away long enough to shuck off his jeans and shoes and socks, then his boxers hit the pile with hers.

Her smile of pleasure drove the flare of hunger inside him to an intensity that bordered on pain. He wanted to take her right then and there, standing up in the bathroom with the steam floating from the shower and cocooning them into its mist.

But she shivered again, and the scent of the salt water in her hair reminded him that she needed warmth and tender care, not to be rushed by his savage needs.

So he took her hand, kissed her fingers, then led her into the shower. The warm water cascaded down her like rain running down a sculpted goddess, and he soaped the sponge and bathed her, gently touching every crevice of her body. She arched against him, giving him access, and smiling as her nipples budded beneath his fingers.

He couldn't resist. He turned her around and rinsed her, then lowered his head and licked the pointed tips, sucking gently on one then the other.

"Oh, Parker," she moaned. "That feels heavenly."

He grinned, then lathered her hair, amazed at her beauty and that she was offering herself to him.

Then she gave him the same treatment, running the sponge over his body, pausing occasionally to kiss his scars. Emotions clogged his throat, then she bathed his hard length and he groaned her name, mindless with pleasure.

He grabbed her hand and pulled it away. He couldn't stand any more. When he lost control, he wanted to be inside her, wanted to take her with him when he came.

PARKER'S TENDERNESS moved Grace in a way she'd never been moved before. His hands on her skin felt exquisite, his mouth delicious, the hunger in his eyes so sensual she quivered. She wanted more. Wanted his mouth on her everywhere. Touching, tasting, exploring, driving her wild with passion.

And he complied.

They dried each other off, then he wrapped a big towel around her and carried her to the bed. She flipped down the covers and they fell into the sheets, a tangle of arms and legs and frenzied kisses that brought a moan to her lips.

Their mouths mated while he tortured her body with his fingers, twisting her nipples to hard peaks, tiptoeing across her breasts, down her stomach and into her heat. She spread her legs, welcoming him with a cry of pleasure, and he slid his fingers into her femininity, stroking and massaging her until she clawed at his arms for more.

His lips came next, exploring, tasting, licking and sucking her neck, her breasts, then lower until he dampened the insides of her thighs with his tongue and sank it inside her as he had his fingers. She cried his name, a maelstrom of emotions and sensations bombarding her. Euphoria washed over her in waves as her body convulsed against his onslaught, and her orgasm sent a kaleidoscope of colors dancing through her head.

How she loved this man. Had loved him ever since she'd first seen him fighting for his life in the ER.

How could she ever bear to lose him?

For a moment panic threatened to rob her pleasure, but she shut out everything but the joy of having his mouth and hands on her.

Her skin tingled as he rose above her and gazed into her eyes. His were dark, intense, heady with need, and she suddenly felt vulnerable and exposed knowing that hers probably revealed a wild, primitive passion that she'd never experienced with another man.

She wanted the night to last forever.

He grabbed a condom from the night-stand drawer, rolled it onto his thick length and thrust inside her. He was hard, big, so big that for a moment she thought her body couldn't accommodate him, but he stretched her with his force. Her world spun another hundred and eighty degrees as he filled her, pulled out and thrust inside her again.

"Grace…" His guttural groan embold-ened her and she ground her hips against him, wrapping her legs around his waist to draw him deeper inside her, clawing at his arms as he pounded their bodies together. He was intense, driven, more primitive than any man she'd ever been with, more man than she could take, but she did take him, all of him, and she loved every inch, every second, that he moved inside her, every sound he made as he joined their bodies, every touch of his hands as he jerked her hips up to fill her more completely.

Another mind-boggling orgasm shook her and he caught her cry of pleasure with his mouth, fusing them together as his own body spasmed with release. She clenched his hips with her fingers, holding him inside her, so shaken by the power of their lovemaking that a tear slipped down her cheek and onto the sweat glistening his skin.

She would never forget the night or the way Parker made love to her with his heart and soul. And even though he would probably leave her tomorrow, she would love him forever.

PARKER REELED with emotions and the intensity of his orgasm. He clutched Grace tightly in his arms, breathing in her scent, reveling in the fact that this woman had given herself to him without restraint.

And he had taken with a fierceness that vibrated down to his soul.

He never wanted to let her go.

But tomorrow they had to face reality. She'd be forced to confront Frank, relive the horror of knowing he'd betrayed her family in the worst way.

And he'd have to return to work. Forget that he cared for her, that for a moment in time he'd had the woman of his dreams in his arms.

She pressed a kiss to his chest and stroked his arm, and his heart squeezed. Bradford had found a way to keep the love of his life.

Could Parker possibly do the same— find a way to make it work with Grace so that he didn't have to tell her goodbye?

Chapter Nineteen

They made love again and again during the night. Each time seemed more intense, more tender, more emotional.

Parker had never stayed all night with a woman. Had never had the desire to wake up with one in his arms. But when he awakened with Grace curled next to him, her hand pressed against his chest, her lips so close to his that he had to have another taste, he knew he had to try to make this relationship work.

She opened her eyes and gazed into his, and he thought he saw love shining back. His heart swelled, and he tucked a strand of hair behind her ear, then kissed her cheek. She moaned and rubbed against him, and his body hardened again. He would never stop wanting Grace.

A smile lit her eyes, and she threaded her fingers in his hair and he melded her lips with his. A second later he'd kissed his way all over her body, then slid inside her once more. Together they rocked and stroked each other, the early morning sunlight casting a golden halo across her face as she came apart in his arms.

He moaned his own release, meeting her cry of pleasure with his own, then rolled her sideways into his embrace and pressed her head against his chest.

He hesitated only a moment, then murmured, "Marry me, Grace."

She tensed, and he held his breath. "Grace?"

"Parker…"

He pulled back, looked into her eyes. They were lying face to face, their heads touching, bodies still slick with perspiration and the scent of their lovemaking. She couldn't turn him down.

"Parker, I…love you."

His breath whooshed out. "I love you, too."

She closed her eyes, then a tear trickled down her cheek and she pulled away and sat up, dragging the covers over her breasts. Panic squeezed his chest. She was shutting down, shutting him out.

"But I can't marry you, Parker."

He reached for her, but she shook her head, and anger mounted on top of panic. "I don't understand. You said you love me. I love you."

"It's not that simple." Grace's voice cracked as she stood and began searching for her clothes. The ones from the night before were ruined, so she plowed through her suitcase.

He vaulted off the bed and caught her arm, then forced her to look at him. "What's going on, Grace? You can't make love to me the way we did and then just walk away."

"Don't tell me you've never slept with a woman and left the next day?"

Anger churned in his stomach. "Yeah, I have. But I didn't just sleep with you. It was more and you know it, Grace."

She bit down on her lip. "It's not that easy, Parker."

"Then help me understand," he said between clenched teeth.

"I've lost everyone I've ever loved to the job," Grace cried. "I vowed I'd never put myself through that agony again." When she turned, turmoil shadowed her eyes. "I want a family, Parker. I want kids and a husband who will come home to me at night. One I won't have to lie awake wondering if he's dead or alive."

Parker's throat closed. "I'm sorry, Grace. I don't know how to be anything else but a cop."

She walked back to him then, pressed a hand to his cheek. "I know, and I wouldn't ask you to leave your job. It's as much a part of you as nursing is to me." She paused, twisted her fingers together. "But I just can't live with it, Parker. I wish I could, but I can't."

GRACE DRAGGED herself away from Parker while she could. Hurt strained his features, but she didn't have the courage to retract her words. She'd barely survived her parents' death and the loss of her brother—she wouldn't be able to exist if she lost Parker to the job.

His phone rang, and she raced to the shower while he answered it. When she emerged, he handed her a cup of coffee, then ducked into the shower himself. Her heart sank at the memory of them bathing each other the night before. She would never get to see him naked again. Feel his arms around her. His body inside her.

But she'd have to go on. She always had…

The next two hours passed in a hushed daze as she and Parker drove to the police station, but she reminded herself she'd done the right thing.

"That call," Parker said. "Kelly Johnson died during the night. Frank's ready to talk."

She nodded, grief for Frank's lost daughter adding to the emotions churning through her as she entered the interrogation room.

Along with grief, guilt clouded his

ruddy features. She wanted to hate him, to lash out at him with her fists, but all she could do was stare at him with pity and hurt.

"I'm sorry about Kelly," she said quietly as she claimed a chair across from him. She had to sit—her knees were buckling too badly to stand.

"Grace, I'm so sorry." Frank's eyes teared up. "I don't know what they told you—"

"The man who tried to *kill* me yesterday said to ask you about my parents' murder. You and your friends." She gestured toward Parker. "And Detective Kilpatrick told me the rest, that the three of you were taking bribes. That you hired Juan Carlos to kill me. I suppose he shot Bruno, too."

He coughed into his hand. "He wasn't supposed to kill you," Frank said in a high-pitched voice. "Only scare you off from asking questions."

"But you had my parents murdered. How could you, Frank?"

"It wasn't me, not exactly," Frank said, although guilt roughened his words.

"I…was desperate back then. My wife was gone and Kelly's medical expenses were sky-high, eating me alive. I…they were going to deny treatment, postpone one of her surgeries if I couldn't pay. That might have cost her her life." He coughed again. "So I did take money, and then I found the others were, too, and I guess it didn't seem so bad. But your father discovered we were accepting bribes, and he threatened to expose us all. They would have sent me to jail and who would have taken care of Kelly then?" He dropped his head into his hands. "I couldn't leave her all alone."

"So you hired someone to kill my folks to save yourself?"

"To save Kelly," Frank insisted. "And I didn't hire them. I tried to talk to your father. I begged him, pleaded with him…" His voice broke. "But McKendrick was impatient. When I found out his plan, I tried to stop him, but it was too late."

Remorse laced his voice, but still he'd been involved and had covered it up.

"So when Bruno dug too close to the

truth, you had him shot in the head just like they were?"

"No." Frank jumped up and paced across the small room, his shoes clicking on the floor. "Not me. I didn't have your brother killed. I swear it."

"Then McKendrick did?"

"No, he's too ill, he barely knows his own name."

"Bart Yager?" Parker asked.

Frank huffed a tired breath. "I don't know. You'll have to ask him yourself." He turned to Grace, imploring her to believe him. "I swear, sweetheart, I had nothing to do with Bruno's death."

"Don't ever call me sweetheart again," Grace snapped.

He winced, and she wanted to apologize, to believe him, but the shock and pain of knowing he'd stood by while her parents' killer went free for years kept her from softening. Too much hurt and anger churned in her chest.

So much that she got up and walked out of the room, knowing she'd never think of Frank as family again.

PARKER SENSED that the last few days had been too much on Grace. She looked like a delicate flower petal about to break beneath the wind. But even as he followed her out of the room, the fact that she'd turned down his proposal stirred his pain as if a knife was digging into his chest. He'd never thought he'd give his heart to anyone, but to have her throw his love back in his face had ripped him in two.

Grace needed peace, needed a future that included happiness and life without being tainted by crime. She'd never have that with him, and she knew it.

And he loved her so damn much that he wanted her to be happy. So he had to let her go.

"I'm going to question Yager," he said as they met up in the bullpen.

She nodded, but Bradford stepped up to join them before she could say anything else.

"The ME finished Bruno's autopsy report. You won't believe what they found."

Grace spun toward Walsh. "What?"

"He had tissue removed, tissue that he

hadn't voluntarily donated. So did several of the other corpses that went missing. We're bringing in the assistant ME now for questioning. Apparently he signed off on the bodies."

"So someone was stealing the tissue?" Grace asked.

Bradford nodded. "Apparently whoever did it sold it to tissue banks to make a profit, but in the process, some of it was contaminated."

"You think it was this assistant ME?"

"It's possible. Or someone could have paid him to turn a blind eye," Bradford said. "Anyway, I just thought you'd want to know."

"I'm going to question Yager now about Bruno's death," Parker said.

Bradford agreed to sit in, and Parker turned to Grace. "One way or another we're going to get a confession out of the man, so you'll have your answers about your parents and your brother."

"Thank you, Parker, for everything you've done for me."

He nodded, wishing he could do more.

But the only thing left was to tie up the loose ends of the case so she could move on.

"I STILL CAN'T believe Frank betrayed my father, then pretended to be a family to me and Bruno."

Parker gave her a sympathetic look. "I'm sorry, Grace. But if it helps, I do think he cares for you. I think he just got in over his head."

She gave a clipped nod. Part of her understood Frank's desperation over taking care of Kelly, but another part ached so badly that she could barely breathe. She needed space, time away from Frank and from Parker.

Because even though she'd refused his proposal, she wanted him more than ever.

"Take the car, go home, get some rest," Parker said. "I'll finish questioning Yager, and let you know when I get his confession."

She bit down on her lip. "But how will you get home?"

"Walsh can drive me."

"Thank you, Parker. I...I am tired." Tired of fighting her feelings for him, of thinking about the night before and how close they'd been at his cabin, of thinking about how lonely her bed would feel tonight at home without him in it.

Tired of imagining how her father would feel if he knew his own partner, the man he'd trusted to watch his back, was partly responsible for his death.

"I think I will go," Grace said. "Call me and let me know what happens."

Parker nodded, and Grace rushed out the door. A few minutes later she parked at her home on Tybee and went inside, but reminders of her family assailed her inside the house. The quilt her grandmother had made from her mother's Sunday dresses. The picture of her and Bruno when he'd graduated from the police academy sat on the sideboard. The one of her parents and Bruno and her when they'd gone crabbing one day and all come home with dozens of mosquito bites....

After hearing what Frank had said, their loss was as raw as if it had just happened. She was supposed to take care of Bruno, but he'd died. And even in death, someone had desecrated his name by making his death look like a suicide. Then others had violated him by removing tissue that he hadn't willingly donated.

She wanted those people caught, as well. They had to pay.

Furious and eager to talk to the ME herself, she dashed back to the car, swung it around and drove toward the hospital. Dr. Whitehead had performed transplants. Did he know who was responsible for stealing the tissue?

Could he possibly have known that it had been obtained illegally?

By the time she arrived at the hospital, her palms were sweating. Surely, Wilson hadn't known….

She slung her purse over her shoulder as she entered the facility, then she took the elevator to the third floor and headed toward Dr. Whitehead's office. He normally scheduled surgeries for the morning, so she hoped he'd be free. Then she'd talk to the ME.

She spoke to two of the nurses, then turned the corner and stopped at Dr. Whitehead's door. Heated voices echoed from the inside, and she paused, hand on the doorknob.

"You need to leave," Wilson shouted.

"I'm not going anywhere," the man said in a menacing tone.

She flinched. Why was Wilson so upset? Was the man one of the victims of the contaminated tissue?

"Get out now!" Wilson snapped.

"No."

Alarmed, Grace knocked, but a strained silence followed. She knocked again, then fear twisted her stomach and she opened the door and burst inside. "Wilson—"

He was slumped backward in his chair, his eyes dazed, his mouth slightly open as if he were trying to speak but couldn't. Suddenly something sharp pierced her neck, and she realized that the man who'd been arguing with Wilson had been hiding behind the door.

And he'd just given her some kind of injection.

Her legs buckled as she tried to see the man's face, but the room spun sickeningly and she felt herself falling, the world fading as she hit the floor and blacked out.

Chapter Twenty

Parker strode into the interrogation room to question Yager. He'd been surprised the police had gotten the man to the station so quickly, but Bradford informed him that Yager had been in Savannah. Which told him that his and Grace's earlier visit had shaken up the man and that he'd been en route to talk to Frank, to formulate a plan to continue their cover-up.

Armed with that theory, he gritted his teeth as he faced the man. "Mr. Yager, we meet again so soon."

Bart leaned on the table, fingers drumming. "You're barking up the wrong tree," Yager said, although his tone vibrated with nerves.

"Really?" Parker arched a brow and

planted his hip on the edge so he could look down at the man. "Why is that?"

"What did Frank tell you?"

Parker grimaced. "The truth about what happened with the Gardeners."

Yager stared at him deadpan, then released a ragged breath. "That was a long damn time ago."

"Yeah, and Grace suffered every minute since she saw her parents brutally murdered."

Regret flashed in the man's eyes for a nanosecond, but a hardness replaced it seconds later. "I swear, none of us wanted that."

"No, but you stood by and had her parents killed to protect your own asses anyway."

"It wasn't like that. Frank was desperate, I had…bills, a gambling problem."

"And McKendrick?"

"He was just plain greedy, but he's serving his sentence now with Huntington's. And if it makes any difference, Frank has grieved for the Gardeners as much as anyone. He tried so hard to make it up to Grace and Bruno—"

"How? And you all did that by hiring Juan Carlos to kill Grace?"

"We didn't do that," Yager argued. "We only wanted to scare Grace, not kill her."

"Because you knew she would find out that you had Bruno murdered?"

Yager shook his head. "No…no, we didn't kill Bruno." He dropped his head forward, his shoulders slumped. "I swear."

Parker grilled the man for twenty more minutes, and although Yager owned up to being an accomplice in the Gardeners' shooting, and conspiring to warn Grace through Juan Carlos, he refused to admit any involvement in Bruno's death. He insisted that Carlos tossing Grace into the sea was his own doing, not his or Frank's.

"Sit tight, Yager, I'll be right back." Parker finally excused himself and met Walsh in Captain Black's office. "I don't get it, he won't cop to Bruno's death. And there's no reason for him not to now, not with the trouble he's already in."

"Maybe he's telling the truth." Bradford folded his arms across his chest. "We just finished questioning that lab assistant at the tissue bank. He confessed that the assistant ME stole the bodies for tissue removal to sell. He'd had a black market business and was making a hefty profit. Rostan, the lab tech at L-Tech, even got in on the action." Bradford hesitated. "And get this, Bruno Gardener was investigating the case."

Parker's heart thumped. "What did he find out?"

"That some of the tissues were being used in experimental research at CIRP."

Parker swallowed hard. "I'll bet Whitehead was in on it."

"His name came up," Bradford said.

A cold knot of fear seized Parker. Whitehead had expressed interest in Grace. He'd thought the man might be in love with her, but what if he'd stayed close to find out if she knew anything about her brother's investigation? What if he'd stayed close to keep her quiet?

"I have to call Grace, warn her," Parker said.

Bradford reached for the doorknob. "We'll do it on the way to the hospital."

Parker nodded, and they jogged outside to Bradford's car. Parker punched in Grace's cell number as his partner started the engine and they sped from the parking lot.

He waited two, three, four, five rings. Adrenaline made his heart race.

"Damn it, she's not answering," he shouted, then dialed her home number but again received no answer.

"Maybe she took a nap," Bradford suggested.

"Swing by her cottage," Parker said. "I have to find out."

Bradford nodded and steered the car onto the causeway. Parker hung up and tried Grace's cell phone again, but it rang and rang until the machine finally clicked on. He left a message warning her that she might still be in danger, to stay away from Whitehead.

"Something's wrong," he said, wiping at the perspiration trickling down his face.

"Which way?" Bradford asked.

Parker gave him directions on the island and they barreled into the drive. As soon as they stopped, Parker vaulted from the car and ran to the door, pounding on it. "Grace, it's Parker. Open up!"

Tension strained his muscles as he listened, but there was no sound inside. Bradford hurried around the house to check the back door and windows, then rushed back.

"There's no sign that anyone's home or that there's been an intruder."

Still, Parker jimmied the door and stormed inside, searching the rooms one by one. But Grace was nowhere in the house.

His phone rang and he headed back outside. "Kilpatrick, it's Black. A call just came in. Dr. Whitehead was attacked at the hospital. He's barely conscious but he told one of the nurses that the assistant ME, Lamar Poultry, has Grace Gardener."

"God…" His breath caught in his throat. "Did Wilson say where he took her?"

"It just happened. They may still be in the hospital."

"We're on our way." He raced to the

car, filling in Bradford as they sped away from Grace's.

He had to find her, save her one more time. He couldn't lose her before he said goodbye.

GRACE TRIED to open her eyes, but the light hurt so badly she closed them again. Her body felt heavy, and she couldn't move her limbs. She must be tied down. Yes, on some kind of table.

A surgical table like they had in the operating rooms.

Or the morgue…

She swallowed the terror and screamed, but the sound that emerged faded into thin air.

Questions bombarded her. Where was she? And who had attacked her?

What about Wilson? Was he alive? If someone had found him and he'd survived, could he tell them where this man had taken her?

The vile scent of death and blood suddenly assaulted her senses and she coughed. Then it hit her—she was in the cold room where they kept the bodies before transporting them to the funeral homes and the morgue.

"You shouldn't have been so nosy," a voice screeched near her ear. "You wouldn't have had to die, but you just wouldn't give it up."

"Give what up?" she whispered hoarsely.

"Trying to find out what happened to your brother."

Her eyes widened. "You? But why?"

"Because he was nosy just like you. We had a good business here, selling tissue. And it wasn't like we were hurting anyone. The tissues were taken from *dead* people—we didn't kill them. We only used their tissues to help others."

"You hurt others with contaminated tissue," Grace hissed. "Some people died."

"And others were healed. The research alone was going to save hundreds in years to come, allow advances in tissue enhancement." His voice trilled in the tense silence. "Even your precious detective benefited. That last tissue he received was chemically enhanced so he healed twice the normal rate expected."

This man was crazy. "But you killed Bruno."

A nasty laugh rumbled from the man. "And made it look like a suicide. Thought it was pretty clever to use the same kind of gun that killed your parents. I knew that would throw off the cops."

And it had.

"At least his tissue helped others," the man crooned. "And so will yours, Grace. I'll make sure of that."

Grace silently grasped for hope. But Parker was busy—he didn't even know she was in trouble.

A tear seeped from her eyes. She didn't want to die. She hated the way she'd left things with Parker.

But she would never get a chance to tell him.

PARKER AND BRADFORD stormed into the hospital, both breathing heavily.

"I'll notify security to close off all exits and to look for the assistant ME."

"I'm going to the ER to question White-head. Maybe he'll know where Poultry took her." He ran down the hall, his heart pounding in his chest. A minute later he pushed his way past two nurses trying to keep him out of the exam room holding Whitehead and charged in.

Whitehead glanced up from the hospital bed, his face as white as the bed-sheets. "Grace…"

"Where is she?" Parker barked.

Whitehead tried to lift his hand, but it flopped back down on the bed as if he had lost control of his limbs.

"He's been drugged," one of the nurses said. "We really need him to rest."

Parker strode straight up to the man's bed. "Poultry was supplying you with tissues for experimentation?"

"We went through the tissue banks," Whitehead said in a hoarse whisper. "Didn't know he was stealing them."

"Yeah, right."

"True," Whitehead said, then lapsed into a cough. The nurse glared at Parker, but he refused to back down.

"Where would he take her?" he asked coldly.

"Don't know—"

"Think, damn it. Grace's life depends on it."

Whitehead's eyes widened. "The cold room…basement. It's probably where he stole the bodies before they were transported."

Right. That made sense. He should have thought of it himself, but panic for Grace was clogging his brain.

"Save her," Whitehead said gruffly.

"I will," Parker said.

He raced from the room toward the elevator. A group of people stood waiting, and Parker silently cursed. No time to wait. He darted into the stairwell and raced down the steps to the basement, his boots clicking on cement as he descended two steps at a time. He shoved open the door to the basement, and searched the signs. X-rays and Radiation to the left, the cold room and unit for biohazard disposal to the right. He headed toward the cold room, driven by anger and fear. He had to save Grace, had to be on time.

He couldn't stand it if she died.

The stench of death and chemicals assaulted him as did the cold wave of frigid air from the dark room that lay behind closed doors. He hesitated, listened for a sound, but silence radiated around him as chilling as the air that hit him when he opened the door to the room.

Surprisingly there was no one monitoring the door to check for ID—anyone could go inside. Anyone could get access to these bodies and do what they wanted at will.

He held his breath while he checked the toe tags, but saw none with Grace's name. Still, the man could have falsified her name. Bracing himself, he unzipped the bags and checked them one by one.

Thankfully no Grace.

A scream wrenched the silence, a wail of terror that he recognized as coming from Grace.

He pivoted, decided her cry had come from the neighboring room, so he pushed at the door. But it was locked.

He unholstered his gun and shot the door lock. Once. Twice. Gritting his teeth, he twisted the knob and kicked open the door.

His heart stopped. Grace was tied down to a surgical table and Poultry stood over her, holding a hypodermic in his hand.

Chapter Twenty-One

Poultry jerked his head toward Parker, his face twisting into a snarl. "Going to join us, Detective?"

Parker raised his weapon and aimed. "Put down the needle, Poultry."

"I wasn't going to hurt her," Poultry said with a sick laugh. "Just put her to sleep forever."

"He killed Bruno," Grace whispered hoarsely.

"I know you're the one who's been stealing the bodies," Parker said. "That you removed tissue and sold it to the tissue banks."

Poultry frowned, wild-eyed, as if he might be high. "I'm not going to jail. I'd rather die."

Parker took a step forward. "That can be arranged."

Poultry raised the needle to stab himself, but Parker lunged toward him and knocked it out of his hand with the butt of his gun, then grabbed his arms, spun him around and slammed his face down onto the floor. A second later he jammed his foot on top of Poultry's back, then snapped the handcuffs tightly around his wrists.

"Why didn't you just let me die?" the man cried.

"Because that's the easy way out," Parker growled. "You need to go to prison and pay."

After reading Poultry his rights, he reached for his phone, punched in Bradford's number and told him where they were.

Grace was squirming, struggling to free herself. "Move and I'll shoot you," Parker told Poultry.

His pulse clamored as he rushed to the table and untied the bindings around Grace's wrists and ankles.

"Thank God you got here, Parker. He's crazy..."

"I know, baby." He yanked her into his arms and pressed her head to his chest, rocking her back and forth. His chest ached from an effort to breathe, from knowing he was almost too late. "But he's going to pay now."

Bradford and a security guard burst into the room, quickly assessing the scene. "She all right?" Bradford asked when he saw that the assistant ME was secured.

"Yeah. Do me a favor, get him out of here," Parker growled. "And let's have a CSI team in here to photograph the scene and sweep it for trace. I don't want this guy going free for any reason."

Bradford nodded. "Come on, Poultry. We've got a cell waiting for you."

Parker glanced at the security guard. "If you could confiscate security tapes, that would help."

"Sure thing." The guard hurried out and Parker helped Grace off the gurney. He was still shaking all over from seeing her strapped down.

She clung to his arm, her legs buckling. "Parker…"

"Not here." He picked her up and carried her through the doors, then headed outside. Grace curled against him, her body trembling. He paused in the shadows of the doorway outside, breathing in the night air, then sent a prayer to heaven that he'd made it in time to save Grace.

"I was so afraid I'd lost you," he said, hugging her tight.

She pressed her hand against his chest. "I thought I'd lost you, too."

His gaze met hers, emotions lodging in his throat.

"Where do you want to go from here?" he asked quietly.

She traced a finger along his mouth. His stomach clenched at the emotions darkening her eyes. "Home with you," she whispered.

Relief surged through him. "Are you sure?"

She nodded.

"Are you going to walk away again?"

He breathed deeply. "Because I don't want only one night, Grace."

She shook her head. "No, Parker, no more running."

He kissed her hair. "God, Grace…I was so afraid I'd be too late—"

"But you weren't," she said softly. "You saved me, Parker. You protected me."

"I would have died for you."

"I know." Her voice broke, and she stroked the side of his cheek. "How can I walk away from a man like that?"

His chest ached. "I could think about taking a desk job—"

She pressed a finger to his lips to hush him. "No, you're a cop, that's who you are, just like my brother and father."

"But you said you couldn't marry a cop, couldn't live that life."

"I was wrong." She kissed his jaw. "I couldn't marry anyone else." She traced a finger over his lips. "I realized something when I was trapped in there. I'll always worry about you coming home at night, even if we aren't together."

He kissed her thoroughly, pouring his

heart and soul into the kiss. "Then marry me, Grace? I promise I'll come home to you and love you as long as I live."

She laughed softly. "Yes, Parker, I'll marry you."

He grinned, his chest swelling with hope and dreams for their future. "All right, we're going to have the doctor check you out. Then I'm taking you home."

She clutched his shirt. "Are you sure you don't have to go to the station? Take care of business? Go to physical therapy?"

He shook his head. "Rehab can wait. And Bradford can go to the station. I have more important things to do."

She arched a brow, a teasing smile in her eyes. "Like what?"

"Like take you to bed." He nuzzled her neck and began walking toward the ER. "I'm going to hold you until we both stop shaking, then make love to you until dawn." He kissed her again, this time tenderly, filling the kiss with promises to come.

"Then we'll sleep in each other's arms, wake up and do it all over again."

"That sounds perfect." She sighed and curled into his arms. "I love you, Parker. I will love you forever."

He laid his head against hers. "I love you, too, Grace."

* * * * *

Don't miss Rita Herron's upcoming books of gripping romantic suspense throughout 2008, only from Harlequin Intrigue!

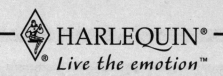

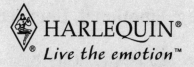

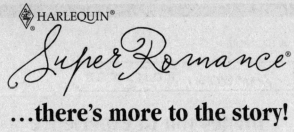
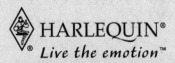

Harlequin® Historical
Historical Romantic Adventure!

*Imagine a time of chivalrous
knights and unconventional ladies,
roguish rakes and impetuous
heiresses, rugged cowboys
and spirited frontierswomen—
these rich and vivid tales will
capture your imagination!*

*Harlequin Historical . . .
they're too good to miss!*

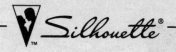

SPECIAL EDITION™

Emotional, compelling stories that capture the intensity of living, loving and creating a family in today's world.

Desire

Modern, passionate reads that are powerful and provocative.

nocturne

Dramatic and sensual tales of paranormal romance.

Romantic SUSPENSE

Romances that are sparked by danger and fueled by passion.